The Lock-Keeper's Cottage
and other stories

The Lock-Keeper's Cottage

and other stories

by Anne Merrick

Cover illustrations by Isobel Davies

First published by Lily Neal 2020
Topsham, UK

Copyright © Anne Merrick 2020

ISBN: 978-0-9956661-5-3

This edition printed and bound by Short Run Press, Exeter, UK

DEDICATION

For Donald and Clare Blackburn

THANKS

Once again, my thanks go to my sister, Isobel Davies, for her help and support and for her hard work on the cover illustrations, and to my editor, Lily Neal. I should also like to thank my late husband, Brian, whose photographs enhance this book.

CONTENTS

FROM MAGDALENA'S KITCHEN

From her kitchen Magdalena could not see the only tree in her garden, nor what lay beneath it. It was many years since she had regretted *that*: so many she could not count them. She rarely thought about it now, and what thoughts she had were brittle, dried out, bereft even of grief.

This room had been her refuge and had come to contain all that was left of her life, absorbing into itself all its lost promise.

"I'm a stupid old woman," she said to her dog, as melancholy threatened. "I might as well mourn those in yonder churchyard, dead of the plague these thousand years since!"

Eeyore, lugubrious as his name, eyed her darkly before settling back into his smelly basket. She shuffled across the floor, her feet in their worn slippers scuffing the dirty flagstones.

"Damned old legs!" she said.

Ninety years old, to be precise. It was high time they carried her away altogether. After placing the kettle on the hob (the electric kettle was long defunct) she crept back to the window. The hump of Pikebury Round stood out clearly against a dove-coloured sky, its chimneys making a jagged frieze above the remains of its encircling wall. It was the only walled village in the kingdom.

"Or should that be *queen*dom?" she said to Eeyore.

Some way outside the village, the church stood like a child banished from the room for bad behaviour. In real-

3

ity, however, it was the village that had moved. When Black Death had stalked the land the whole population of Pikebury had been wiped out and when, centuries later, a new village was gradually built, it was on a site well away from haunted ground, leaving the church stranded.

Through the panes of eighteenth-century glass in her kitchen window the view Magdalena saw was warped and rippled, as if seen through water. Light from the rising sun gleamed on the curve of the river and illuminated the medieval bridge, across which nothing moved. It was too early even for Joe Greenaway, the postman, to be out and about. Beyond the hedge enclosing her garden the water meadows that lay between her cottage and the river were invisible.

"Tiddlers Round, this place is called," Jonathan had said, the day he first brought her to the cottage. "The garden's like a small offspring of the village. A perfect circle! And its high hedge and its isolation, make it the ideal place for visiting you unobserved".

But he had not visited. At least, not after . . .

Magdalena's thoughts skittered away as the kettle whistled, the sound piercing her like a high-speed drill. She raised her hands to cover her ears and, clumsy as she was these days, her elbow brushed the wall, tilting a crudely framed photograph. Herself and Oliver. 1939. She, aged just eighteen, smart in her crisply-ironed Nanny's uniform, Oliver, aged eight, grinning widely, a wing of bright hair flopping over one eye. He was pointing at something out of shot – the photographer himself most likely. His father. Jonathan. *Him . . .*

* * * * *

The early spring day had turned cold. The fire she had lit in the big hearth smouldered with a dour blue flame that scarcely heated the inglenook. Dragging a blanket from beneath a grumbling Eeyore, she wrapped it round herself, nose crinkling at the doggy smell. As she grew warmer, she lapsed into an uneasy sleep where her dreams conjured Oliver out of the murk of the past.

He was her first charge and the only child she had ever had the chance to love. For a Nanny that was a pathetically low score!

Coming to the surface again, she felt along the table for the mug of tea she had made. It seemed to have lost itself among the clutter of books and bills, the vase of dead daffodils, the remains of several suppers, an empty cake tin, Eeyore's dog chain and her house keys. When at last she located it, she saw with surprise that she must have made it hours ago. It had turned an unappetising muddy brown and was stone cold.

She tried to summon the energy to go and put the kettle on again, but the dreams lingered, the melancholy persisted. Against the white noise of the kitchen, the ticking clock, the rustling fire and the dog's faint snores, she kept thinking she heard Oliver's voice, shrill with childish protest.

"Why must you leave me, Nanny?"

"Because . . ." she had said, and then stalled.

"Did you do something bad?"

"Why would you think that?" she had asked.

He had looked long and hard at her, his eyes like chips of blue glass.

"Cook said," he murmured at last, shamefacedly.

Cook. Mary Jane Latimer. Nosy. Mean-minded. Consumer and purveyor of gossip. The more malicious the better . . .

Choked with angry, unshed tears, Magdalena had said nothing and the boy had shrugged.

"Well, anyway," he had said, "*I* don't care! But I suppose God, and Jesus and all that lot might."

* * * * *

In the corner the grandfather clock uttered a wheezing sigh and then struck ten. Joe Greenaway was late this morning. A little wind had got up, rattling the door on its latch and sneaking through the gaps in the old casements. Magdalena shivered and sipped cautiously at the scalding fresh tea she had made. For some reason the past was crowding in on her today, borne on the March wind, perhaps, its breath tainted with the fragile scent of prim-roses. A seasonal hazard.

When she had told him what his son had said, Jonathan at first had laughed. Later he expressed anxiety about what he called, 'the boy's religiosity'. Later still he became angry – with Mary Jane Latimer for being 'a scandal-mongering old witch', with his wife for being 'a stiff-backed Puritan who had never understood a man's needs' and with her, Magdalena, who had been so careless as to conceive a child . . .

* * * * *

A gust of wind puffed smoke back down the chimney. The fire was still sulky: the wood, supplied by Bill Mardon from his farm behind Tiddlers Round, was too green.

"Curse him for a rogue!" Magdalena exclaimed. She staggered up, gathered more logs from the basket, shook them free of spiders and woodlice and set them on the embers.

On just such a day as this her child, a girl, had been born at Tiddlers Round – born and died within the same hour.

"I want to see her," Magdalena had wailed. "Please let me see her!"

But Jonathan had shaken his head, kissed her and spoken soothing words.

"Your labour was too long," he had murmured, "and the child was sickly . . . worse than sickly . . . not . . . not right . . . "

Unpleasing to God, she had thought bitterly. To God and Jesus and all that lot!

"You've been so ill," he said tenderly. "I thought it would upset you. I'm sorry."

But even then she had known he was lying. He was not sorry. He was relieved.

* * * * *

Days later, when she could walk again, he had taken her to see the tiny grave where he had buried their daughter. As she wept herself into silence, he told her how he had dressed the child in the clothes she had made for it – "Such a wonderful needlewoman, you are!" – and how he had placed her in her cradle and wrapped the whole, small, sad bundle in a shawl before committing her to the earth.

"She can rest in peace, here," he had said, leading Magdalena to the ancient apple tree that stood just behind the cottage, "and you will have her close to you, always".

She had remained standing there for hours as her sobs dwindled to harsh, dry hiccups, while the March wind blustered through the boughs and raindrops, caught in a sudden beam of sunlight, scattered like diamonds among the primroses he had planted.

* * * * *

Magdalena stood up as the dog came sniffing round her knees, tail wagging, hoping for his overdue breakfast. Catching her own eye in the mirror above the dresser she thought how her face had collapsed into its wrinkles, how her lips, once 'plump and red as cherries' (so he had claimed) had shrunk to a thin line over her front teeth (all she had left) and how her thin, cropped hair exposed the bony shape of her skull.

"Death's head," she muttered.

Eeyore, seeing her sit down again, looked glum.

Jonathan was long dead – of a heart attack in middle age. He had bought Tiddlers Round as a 'love nest' but had flown it soon after their daughter's birth, weary, no doubt, of her recriminations, her anger and her unremitting sorrow. She had never seen him again.

* * * * *

The postman, thundering at the door, woke her from yet another doze. She had begun to hope that this helpless falling into sleep was the way Death was choosing to take her. If so, she wished he could be left to get on with it!

Crossly, she called that she was coming. Eeyore, who never barked, growled deep in his throat. It took her two full minutes to reach the door and another two to go back for the keys she had left on the table.

The man who greeted her was not Joe Greenaway.

"Sorry, missus," he said as the wind swept a flurry of dead leaves around her feet. "Joe had a bit of an accident this morning. Nothing serious but his van's out of action."

He grinned as he handed her a large, brown envelope. "Looks official," he said cheerily. "Hope it's not a bill – or a summons!"

Magdalena smiled obligingly and slowly wrestled the door shut. Sometime later (had she slept again?) she unearthed her spectacles from the junk on the table, hooked them over her ears, and opened the envelope.

* * * * *

"May I come to see you?" the handwritten note had read.

Among the reams of typing that accompanied them, these were the only words that had made any sense to her at first. Now, hours later, her tired brain scanned the shreds it could recall from the long, confusing letter sent by an unknown solicitor. There had been names she did not know, all jumbled up with names she did.

She reached for the tumbler of brandy she had filled – how many hours ago? – and returned to mull over another sentence that had registered with her.

"We have to tell you that Mr. Oliver Davenport, whom, you may remember, you cared for as a child, has instructed us in his will . . ."

Oliver. Yes. Of course she remembered Oliver.

Magdalena emerged from the trance that had seized her on reading the solicitor's letter and saw with surprise that she was standing under the apple tree. She must have had more brandy than she thought, for she had no recollection of coming out into the garden. To think that Oliver (forever aged eight in her memory) had reached the age of eighty! Her head reeled, and inside it her thoughts flew to and fro like distracted birds.

"Mr. Davenport wished you to know . . ."

The sky had cleared, the wind dropped, and over Pikebury Round smoke from the village chimneys was rising in straight, smudged lines into the still air. She seemed to be wearing Eeyore's blanket like a cloak and she pulled it closer around her. It was going to freeze tonight.

"He requested us to apologise on his behalf . . ."

At her feet her baby's grave lay under its snug quilt of primroses, to which over the years she had added snowdrops, crocuses, winter aconites and miniature daffodils. Today the colours dazzled her eyes.

"He acknowledges that his father, Jonathan Davenport, did you a great wrong . . . but wished you to know that he had only recently come into knowledge of the facts concerning his half-sister, Rose Marie Elgin (née Davenport) now deceased, who was

born on the 15th March, 1940, at Tiddlers Round in the county of . . ."

Magdalena leaned against the tree, and the feel of its gnarled old bark comforted her. It had withstood centuries of wind and weather. Even the great gale that had raked its branches that long-ago March day had failed to fell it. Becalmed and sturdy, it supported her, just as it had always protected the grave . . . the grave that was . . .

". . . moreover, Rose Marie's only child, Jon Davenport Elgin, died two years ago in a car accident . . . therefore we take leave to enclose, from her only surviving relative, her grandson, Oliver David Elgin, a note addressed to you . . ."

Oliver David Elgin. A name never before encountered. A complete stranger.

Eeyore, who was rooting in the undergrowth, gave a sharp yap of excitement. Rabbits, thought Magdalena. She called him away, but as usual he ignored her.

Would the young man look at all like *her* Oliver? Or would his face (and the thought made Magdalena catch her breath) bear traces of resemblance to his grandmother's? Would he look like Rose Marie Elgin? Would she be able to catch in his appearance any hint of the daughter she herself had never seen – never been *allowed* to see?

As if, across the wilderness of the garden, the dog had sensed her bewilderment and her distress, he came back to her at last. He nuzzled her hand, looked up at her with trusting eyes. Magdalena straightened, and glanced down at the grave where *not* her daughter, but her own life, lay buried. Then, her hand on the dog's neck, she turned away.

"*My dear great-grandmother,*" the young man's own note had begun. "*You may imagine how this shocking discovery has . . . Please! . . . May I come to see you?*"

"Come," she said to Eeyore. "We both need to eat. Let's go back indoors."

She knew there were great dangers in challenging fate. But as she stood again at her kitchen window – from where she could see the church, but not the apple tree, nor what lay beneath it – Magdalena, who never prayed, offered up a prayer.

"Please, God . . . and Jesus . . . and all that lot," she said, "help me to keep old Death at bay a little while longer. At least until . . ."

GRANDAD

Bryony was late. The visits to her grandfather at the Forest Glade Care Home were taking longer and longer and this one had been particularly trying. The old man had been more confused than ever. Even his voice had seemed unlike his own. Barely above a whisper one minute, it had swept in a sudden crescendo to a shout the next, startling her out of the trance of thought into which she kept lapsing. Finally, he had wandered off before she could even say goodbye.

Confusion must be contagious, she thought, as she reached her car and inserted the key in the door. It would not turn and after a puzzled moment she realised it was because the door was already unlocked.

"Not like me to leave it that way," she said to herself as she climbed in, throwing jacket and handbag onto the already cluttered passenger seat beside her. "Jam and plaster! – as Grandad would say!"

"That daft expression!" her mother had once said to her. "It's your grandfather's way of saying 'damn and blast it'. Even as a child I thought it was a prissy way of disguising an already mild oath!"

Now it was the rush hour and the road link to the motorway was busy. Mark was going to be furious with her for being late again. Too harassed to listen to anything on CD or radio Bryony talked to herself, rehearsing her anxieties out loud.

"How much worse is it going to get? If Grandad deteriorates any further they won't keep him at Forest Glade. Then where will we be?"

"In the slurry – that's where!"

Concentrating on entering the traffic flow and still absorbed in her own self-questioning, Bryony did not at first register that the voice answering her query came from the back seat of the car. When she did register it, she clenched with momentary fear, her foot slowly depressing the brake, her glance freezing on the rear-view mirror. But all she could see was the lorry pounding up behind her and she was just beginning to relax when the voice spoke again.

"Come on, hurry, or we'll *all* be in the slurry."

The voice, which seemed to come from low down in the car, was husky and gruff, and repeated the line twice more before falling silent.

"Grandad?" she whispered.

"What?" answered the voice.

Oh, God! The old boy must have slipped out of the door at Forest Glade while she had been talking to Jenny, the receptionist, and then climbed into her unlocked car – possibly expecting her to take him somewhere as she occasionally did. Bryony dared not take her eyes off the road, so with one hand she reached back between the front seats and felt about. Sure enough, there was a body on the back seat. Prone but warm, it moved as she touched it.

"Get off," said the voice. "That tickles!"

"Oh, Grandad!" she said, withdrawing her hand. "What on earth are you doing there? You can't come with me today. We'll have to turn round . . . but there's no exit for five miles . . . and I'm already so late!"

"Late, late, for a very important date," the voice chanted.

"Yes. As it happens," she said. It unnerved her, talking like this to someone she could not see "Please, Grandad," she said. "Sit up. You need to put your seat belt on."

"Fiddlesticks!" he said. "Hey, diddle diddle, the cat and the fiddle, the cow jumped over the moon!"

She heard him shift and change position, but he still did not sit up.

"I'm going to have to take you back," she said.

"Back to the old folks at home," he warbled.

Bryony giggled and heard him echo her, snuffling and gurgling until he started to cough. She was tempted to say, "You're a naughty boy, Grandad," but that would be demeaning, she thought, outrageous. Whatever was happening to him, he was a grown man, she told herself: well-informed – well-travelled – well-read – generous, kind and wise. That man was still there somewhere, trapped in the prison of his dying brain . . . lost . . . wandering . . . bewildered.

Tears threatened her and she said, "Tell me about when you were young." It was a request that always in the past had produced stories. But today the silence in the back of the car grew longer and longer.

Ahead of her she could see that the traffic in all lanes was slowing down. "Please don't let there be a hold-up!" she murmured. "Not now! We're still two miles from an exit . . ."

"When I was young . . ." her grandfather's voice suddenly broke into her thoughts again. It had sunk to a hoarse whisper, scarcely audible above the swish and rumble of tyres on tarmac. "It was long, long ago . . ."

"Yes. Yes, I know. But tell me . . . tell me about when you used to go dancing."

"Ha!" he shouted. "Dance, dance, wherever you may be, for I am the Lord of the Dance, said he . . ."

"You were a good dancer, weren't you Grandad?"

The traffic had slowed to below thirty so she risked twisting round to look at him, but he had pulled her travelling rug right over him. No wonder his voice was muffled. Instead of answering her he began to hum, before suddenly saying, loud and clear, "She was the light of my life!"

"Who was?" she encouraged him. "You mean Grandmother? Is that how you met her? Did you go dancing together?"

"Together," he said. "Whatever the weather. And whether the weather was weather or not . . ."

There did not seem to be an accident ahead. No police sirens, no ambulance shrieking up from behind – but the triple line of vehicles had now come to a total halt. Her grandfather had gone quiet again and in the quietness Bryony thought about her grandmother. Even in old age she had been beautiful, her face scarcely lined, her cheek-bones high and prominent under wide grey-green eyes, eyes that to Bryony always seemed sad even when she smiled.

"But I can't imagine her dancing," she said aloud. "She seemed too serious, somehow. Too stately . . ."

"No one is what they seem," said the old man, coming unexpectedly back into the conversation.

"Oh, surely! I should have thought . . ."

"Thought is free . . ."

"Yes, but . . ."

"Yes but! It turned out she was a trollop. A strumpet. A veritable whore of Babylon."

Shocked into silence, Bryony changed gear clumsily and the car jolted forward.

"No, no," she protested. "That can't be right. You must be mixing her up with someone else, Grandad!"

There was a pause and then his voice emerged full throttle for a moment.

"Stop calling me Grandad!" he bellowed. "I'm not your Grandad!"

"Of course you are! Of course you are." She tried to sound soothing and amused at the same time.

"My mother was your daughter, Jane. Remember?" she continued. "So that makes you . . ."

"A diddly doo," he yodelled. "My wife was a trollop, my daughter a bastard. So that makes *you* I don't-know-*who* . . ."

Speeds were picking up and the first blue exit sign was visible ahead. Bryony felt sick.

"Don't know who," repeated the old man. "A diddly doo . . . a diddly doo . . ."

"Please stop it, Grandad," she pleaded.

She could hardly bear the sound of his voice. This grandfather, whom she had loved and respected all her life (even as he retreated from reality, became awkward and sometimes aggressive), this man she knew to be utterly honest, whose coarsest words were 'jam and plaster' and whose devotion to his gentle and graceful wife had been legendary! Dear lord!

His voice petered out at last and minutes later she heard him snoring. But as she left the motorway and started to negotiate the busy city streets her own thoughts nagged on and on. From what dreadful swamp in her grandfather's muddled brain had this reptile idea been dredged? Was it simply a delusion of his illness? Or, heaven forbid, was it an actual memory? Was it false – or was it *true*?

"A diddly doo . . . a diddly doo . . ."

As she turned into the driveway of the Forest Glade Care Home, the nonsense words trickled from under the blanket as though they had sung their way through his dreams ready to rhyme with her own. Bryony tumbled out of the car, knees shaking, one hand already searching for her mobile to ring Mark, when a police car drew up behind her. Of course! There was probably already a search on for her grandfather. She should have rung Forest Glade when she was stationary on the motorway . . .

Jenny was at the door before her, but as Bryony started to speak, the receptionist gestured for her to wait a moment, and then called out to the policeman, "Thank goodness you're here! The old man's been missing for over an hour. We've searched the house and grounds but there's no sign of him anywhere . . ."

"It's OK, Jenny," said Bryony. "My grandfather's in my car. He's quite safe. *I've* got Grandad."

She stuttered on the beloved name, the name that might not now be applicable, and Jenny looked at her blankly.

"Your grandfather?" she said. "Mr. Ingrams?"

"Yes. Of course. I'm so sorry . . ."

The constable, climbing the slope towards them, breathed heavily, portentously.

"But that's not possible," said Jenny. "Mr. Ingrams is here, having his tea."

Bryony felt the world make a slow revolution. She turned to look at her car where a wizened but grinning face now appeared at the rear window.

"Why!" cried Jenny. "There he is! It *is* our missing resident! Welcome back, Mr. Gladhill!"

"Ah," said the policeman. "I take it the problem has resolved itself?"

Then he and Jenny both looked in consternation at Bryony as she began to laugh hysterically.

"Oh, jam and bloody plaster!" she gasped, when at last she could speak. "Would you believe it? The old man was right! He said he wasn't . . . and about *that*, at least, he was *absolutely right*. He's *not* my Grandad . . . "

MERMAIDS

Our Lizzie said that there were mermaids in the cove at Abernant. It was the sort of thing she often said. Mam glared at her and told her not to tease me.

"Full of daft fancies, you are," she added as she peeled the potatoes for our dinner. "It'll get you into trouble one of these days."

Lizzie tossed her head so that sparks seemed to fly from the smouldering red of her hair. Her brown eyes were defiant.

"Well, there are," she insisted. "I've seen them."

At that time I must have been – what? – five, or six years old? – and I clung to Lizzie like the ivy to our house wall. In the grey, unadorned dailyness of our lives she appeared to me as an exotic bird; piping strange songs, fluttering brilliant feathers, always in flight.

"You want to see them, boyo?" she said to me.

Of course. Of *course* I wanted to see them.

"Come on, then," she said, stretching out her fingers and taking my hand. Her long skinny legs covered the ground faster even than Dewi Lloyd's could. As I panted along in her wake I remarked how easily they could carry her away from trouble.

"Oh, trouble!" she said as we reached the sandy path that led down to the sea. "We'll always have that! Because we're *outcasts* in this village. We've got no Dad, we don't wear shoes and our clothes come out of everybody's ragbags. So they can feel good when they pay our Mam a pittance for doing their laundry!"

I glanced down at my own bare feet as they trotted along beside her, making the path slide backwards beneath me, squidging the sand up between my toes. I decided I liked them the way they were, and that I didn't *want* shoes. And that I'd rather have toes than a tail.

"What do the mermaids look like?" I asked. "Have they got golden hair?"

"Wait and see," said Lizzie, tugging my hand. I sensed she was in a hurry to be off on another of her adventures. Mainly these were to do with the pirates who hid in Mr. Probert's barn in the daytime and came out to revel on the beach at night. Or sometimes she went looking for the handsome highwayman who roamed Fforest Tywyll, taking the money – or the lives – of any traveller who ventured across the heath at night.

"He buries the gold *with* the bodies," Lizzie said, "at Brynmawr Cross. Where in olden times they used to hang the highwaymen and leave them dangling in chains until they rotted. Good tactics, see? No one would dare to search for the loot *there* because they'd be too scared of the ghosts."

I would be scared of them too. I was scared of all the ghosts. Our Lizzie said the whole village was as full of phantoms as of people.

"They always come out at the dark of the moon," she explained, "and make mischief among the living. Getting their own back for being dead. That's why Megan the Milk was born lacking, and why Idris Jenkins has warts all over his face. And how Maggie Jones managed to lure our Dad away too, I daresay . . ."

This was the only one of Lizzie's stories I doubted. That's because the story of our Dad kept changing. Sometimes he had been kidnapped by fairy folk and might come back one day, years younger than Mam, younger even than us, and he'd sit down and ask for his tiffin just as if he'd never been away. Sometimes he had dived off the cliffs above the cove and then swum all the way to Ireland, and once he had joined the pirates and gone sailing the seven seas until he was captured by the excise men and thrown into the dungeon under Caer Ddu Castle, where he was still languishing.

At the time she told each story I believed it utterly. There was something about the way she told them: the way her brown eyes flashed with anger or sorrow or laughter as the story demanded, the conviction in her voice and the precision of the details. Occasionally she would make them even more real by illustrating them, sketching with a stick in the sand or drawing coloured pictures on the wall of our bedroom with chalk she could wash off before our Mam saw them.

Once, when I'd been specially troubled by a variation in her story of Dad, I risked asking Mam.

"Did our Dad *really* get swallowed by a Great White Whale," I quavered, "out in the bay when he was fishing?"

Mam straightened up and pushed strands of rusty hair out of her eyes.

"*Neno'r nefoedd!*" she exclaimed. "I suppose that's one of Lizzie's lies!"

She drove the wooden dolly hard into the steaming tub, screwing it into the ballooning folds of Mrs. Probert's sheets as if she'd like to kill them.

"Well, here's the truth, my lad," she said tersely. "Your Tad was a RAT. A rat with a roving eye – and Maggie Jones was the Great White Whale that swallowed him!"

But Mam's answer confused me even further. Inside my head I kept seeing a giant rat with one huge, grey, *revolving* eye. And except for the tufts of hair on its head it looked nothing like the Dad I remembered. The whole thing unnerved me, and I did not ask again . . .

As Lizzie dropped my hand and raced out from between the dunes I could see the shining seethe of the sea. The sun was setting fire to the waves and bright bubbles of light fizzed to the horizon. When I was very little – and Dad still there – he had once taken me down to the cove on just such a day as this and, sweeping his hand across the dazzle of the sea, he'd said, "That's better than any dragon's hoard, *cariad*! More precious than a pirate's chest of treasure. The sun and sky belong to us all – and the sparkles on the sea are our jewels. While we have these we will never be poor."

Now, as I followed Lizzie out on to the sand, I decided that *he* must have been a liar, too. As well as being a rat with spinning eyes . . .

Lizzie threw herself down and stared into the glitter on the water. Above us seagulls drifted, slicing the air with wings like silver cutlasses, mewing like cats.

"Listen," said Lizzie, reaching for my ankle and pulling me down beside her. "They're calling to the mermaids."

I squeezed up my eyes, a trick I had found helped me to see farther, and gazed at the tumble of rocks where the high tide foamed and fretted.

"Where?" I urged her. "Where are they? Show me!"

"Look," she said, pointing. "Look! They're waving to us. Can't you see their green hair streaming in the surf like seaweed, their tails curled around the rocks and their scales shimmering with emeralds and sapphires? And listen . . . listen . . . can't you hear them singing?"

I screwed my eyes even tighter. Concentrated until my head ached. And there, scattered all across the sun-glazed rocks, I saw them. Mermaids. Veiled in rainbows, sequinned with sea spray. Smiling. Beckoning . . .

And beneath the deep-voiced boom and roar of the waves rushing onto the shore, I heard their siren song . . .

THE BORDER

The border lay about two hundred metres from The Outpost. That was the name of the cottage on the outskirts of the village to which, long ago, Sophie had come as a bride.

At that time the border had been a mere mountain track marking the boundaries of two countries which shared a language and a history of largely peaceful co-existence punctuated by occasional minor hostilities. Although constantly encroached upon by a scrub of thorn, hazel and birch and by the ubiquitous furze bushes that made the whole hillside a glory of gold in the spring, the track was kept open by the people who came and went over it just as they would with any pathway through the wilderness.

Then, shortly after Sophie was made an early widow, long-standing disputes over land ownership and over religious and political differences had erupted into war. And in spite of opposition from the people on both sides, a fence was erected along the whole length of the border.

Close to The Outpost, the ancient chapel that Sophie had once attended straddled the frontier and became part of the defences. Reduced to a partial ruin by skirmishes between fence-builders and protesters, it stood neglected and forlorn, only its squat stone tower unscathed. The iron bell that still hung in the aperture at its summit had once summoned people from both countries to worship.

Now it was silent unless the wind blew hard from the east, when it would sometimes clang with an erratic, doleful sound.

One limpid day in early May with the gorse ablaze beyond her garden and the crimson camellia against her house wall in full bloom, Sophie was standing at her bedroom window. She was staring with wincing repulsion at the ugly mesh of steel wire that for many years now had cut across her view. Suddenly she heard unaccustomed noises from below: a muted snapping sound as of green twigs breaking, followed by rustling and then the distinct slap of footsteps on her flagstone path. As she looked down a child appeared. A boy. Maybe ten years old. Ragged. Red-haired. And clutched in his fist was a bunch of her precious camellia flowers.

Sophie struggled to release the rusted catch on her window.

"Hey!" she shouted, leaning out.

But the boy dodged through her gate and in seconds had disappeared into the scrub. How had he found his way into her garden? For of one thing, Sophie was certain. The thief did not come from her side of the wire. That bright chestnut hair curling onto his shoulders! No child in the village – or in the wider neighbourhood – had such luxuriant locks . . .

* * * * *

Over the next year or two, the war between Sophie's country and the nation on the other side of the border intensified. Further up country, where there were large centres of population, the fence was attacked over and over again. Refugees and fighters alike flocked through. The fence was renewed, re-enforced and, finally, patrolled. Even in the mountains, soldiers appeared. In twos and threes, with their AK rifles prominent, they regularly tramped the border. From time to time they would pause near The Outpost to light cigarettes and smoke or to mutter into their mobiles. They stared boldly through the rusting network at Sophie's pretty garden, their eyes hard and indifferent. They never spoke to her. Once during that time one of them climbed on to the roof of the chapel. He struck the iron bell with the butt of his rifle, setting it swinging, the notes jangling harshly in the quiet air. His companions cheered as he stuck a small national flag into a crevice in the roof.

It was sometime soon after this incident that Sophie encountered the boy once more. It was spring again, her camellias again in flower. A patrol had recently passed and she had taken the opportunity to stroll down to the chapel. She was not afraid of the soldiery, having decided that at her age death in some form could not be far off, but she hated the exposure. The day was mild and drizzly, mist softening the hills, muting all colour. As she approached the hole in the church wall where the door had once stood, she heard stifled sounds of distress coming from inside. Careful on the tumbled stones and broken spars of wood, she entered the dim interior. Pigeon droppings were splattered everywhere from their roosting places in the rafters. The whole place stank of them and of damp and decay. As her eyes adjusted, Sophie saw the boy crouched against a shattered tomb in the north aisle. The same boy. The same red hair. The same gangly limbs – but taller. He struggled to his feet.

"It's all right," said Sophie quietly. "I'm not going to hurt you."

"I'm hurt already," he said. His voice, on the verge of breaking and thickened by tears, veered between a squeak and a growl.

"How hurt?" she asked, moving closer.

He held out his right hand. On the back of it Sophie saw a jagged cut running from knuckle to wrist. Blood ran down his fingers and dripped on to the stones. She was reminded of the flowers he had stolen, their crimson petals scattering on her path. Her heart, hardened by personal sorrows and the years of conflict, softened.

"Come," she said. "I live close by. I will deal with that."

* * * * *

He was with her for, what – an hour? Less perhaps. She washed his wound, lathered it in antiseptic and bound it tightly. It needed stitches, but at the mere mention the boy threatened to run. She gave him a bowl of soup and a hunk of fresh bread and he ate as if starving. He said very little but she learned enough to know that he had crossed the border through a tunnel he had discovered when looking for food. A rotten tree stump, rich with fungi, had partially blocked the entrance to an old vault. The damage to the building had left an underground gap between the vault and the chapel wall, through which the boy had crawled.

"It was scary," he said. "Scrabbling about in the dark. Among the bones!"

Although she pressed him, he would not tell her his name, nor the name of the village on the far side of the border from which he came.

"My husband was born over there," she murmured. But the boy was not interested. He admitted that on his earlier foray, he had taken her 'roses.'

"For my Gran," he said, his eyes downcast. "'Cause she looked after me."

"They're actually camellias," Sophie said. "But I'll *give* you a bunch this time. To take for her."

"She's dead," he grunted. "Silly old fool. I'm glad to be shut of her . . ."

Sophie shivered. She brought a cake from her pantry and tucked it into his backpack. He grinned. "That'll buy me a smoke or two," he said.

His eyes, the colour of dark sherry, were beautiful but deadened by suffering and deprivation.

"Who looks after you now?" asked Sophie.

"I do," he said.

* * * * *

The years passed. Sometimes Sophie thought about the boy, usually when her camellias were in flower and always with a haunting sense of sadness. Love, she thought, had died in him before he was old enough to know what love was.

The war between her country and his spread. Other nations entered the fray and the mountains were no longer spared the battles. There was the constant roar of planes overhead; the thunderous comings and goings of tanks; artillery and cannon fire near and far. Incursions of rival armies over the border left the fence mangled and the chapel reduced to rubble. Sophie fled from The Outpost and took refuge in the heart of the village.

Later, with even that under direct attack, she hobbled in company with those still left alive along the one road where exit was still briefly possible. Burdened with her few belongings and hampered by age, she struggled to keep up. Behind them, they knew, ruthless warriors would be in pursuit. By the third daybreak, Sophie was alone, resting for a moment in the shelter of a thorn bush as crooked as herself. In the distance she heard the pounding of boots on tarmac and minutes later, in the dawn twilight, she found herself looking up at a young soldier. His khaki uniform was encrusted with mud, his cap missing, his sherry brown eyes unblinking.

"Ah!" she murmured. "So it's you!"

For if the eyes were not enough, there was his hair, cropped now but still richly red and curly. And there was the long, jagged, purple scar on the back of the hand that held his rifle.

The boy gave no sign of recognition. He simply jerked his head in the direction she had been travelling and nudged her firmly – but gently – with the barrel of his gun.

CURIOUS

"It's a curious object –" says the girl. She regards him quizzically out of large pale blue eyes. "– and if you don't mind me saying so, *you* seem exceptionally curious too. I have never been asked so many questions about anything!"

Geraint sets down the streaked and misty glass bowl he has been examining. There is something about the girl that reminds him of his mother – not least her use of the word 'curious' in both its meanings.

"Sorry," he says. He is suddenly aware of how long he has been prowling around the shop. "It's my besetting sin," he adds, "my 'satiable curiosity."

The girl looks blank and Geraint stumbles on for a minute explaining how the phrase comes from a story his mother used to read to him – and how it had sort of stuck to him. She smiles politely, clearly not interested, and he decides it's time to go.

"By the way," he says as he reaches the door, "I think the bowl is genuine Roman glass . . ."

He strides down the High Street. He thinks briefly about the girl. Remembers his mother. He recalls especially the way she worried about his 'satiable curiosity and where it might lead him. Intellectually, she approved of his driving need to know everything about everything. Maternally, she feared it would be the end of him. On his bedroom wall hung an illuminated text she had painted, in which, among the words *Curiosity Killed The Cat* she had

45

sketched witty and brightly-coloured pictures of various disasters.

"But the one she missed," Geraint reflects with a wry smile, "is the one that really did almost do for me!"

* * * * *

As an only child he had been rather solitary – but happy enough as he explored his surroundings, searching for birds' nests, buried artefacts, interesting routes from home to elsewhere and anything that shed light on the history, geography or anthropology of his neighbourhood. By the time he was nine these inquisitive adventures had led to him 'going missing' on numerous occasions. Usually his mother or a kindly neighbour tracked him down, but sometimes the police had to be called and they would retrieve him, delivering him home with a patient smile and yet another dire warning.

Then, two days after his tenth birthday and on the last day of the summer holiday, he had wandered farther than usual and arrived at the edge of the town where the suburbs petered out into a scrubby wilderness that was not quite countryside. It was here that he had found the house.

Hidden behind a ragged copse of ancient trees it was not visible from the road, and he would not have seen it except that as he approached a gap in the woodland, a car pulled into it. The car stopped and disgorged a noisy family of four children, two adults and a dog. The dog bounded off, barking, and the family followed, laughing and jostling each other as they disappeared along what he then saw was an overgrown driveway. Curious as ever, Geraint went after them.

To his childish eyes the house seemed huge: a gothic villa built no doubt for some wealthy Victorian industrialist. Flanked by two round turrets with high conical roofs, its red brick walls were cloaked in Virginia creeper that was just beginning to flame into autumn colour. From one turret rose a flagpole that still sported a tattered shred of flag. On the other a weather vane, shaped like a dragon, creaked slowly round in the shifting wind. The upper windows glittered blankly in the late sun, while the lower ones were sealed – boarded up and blind. Geraint was enthralled.

By the time he reached the flight of cracked stone steps that led to the front door there was no sign of the family, but the massive door stood ajar. Geraint slipped inside.

* * * * *

In his memory the next hour is a blur. He knows he enjoyed an elaborate game of his own as he dodged into empty rooms, squeezed into cupboards and stood rigid and unbreathing in shadowy corners, while the other children rollicked all over the house. From scraps of shouted conversation, he gathered that they were coming to live there. In one of the upper turret rooms where he crouched behind a dusty velvet curtain, he heard one of the smaller ones say, "I'm having this room for my own!"

"Oh, no, you're not," contradicted another voice. "I'm the oldest so I'll get to choose first, and it's mine!"

"Ugh!" shrieked the first one. "There's a dead rat in the fireplace!"

"I don't like it," quavered an infant voice. "It's dirty and spooky and it smells!"

Bored eventually with his game, Geraint climbed higher until he reached the attics where there was enough junk from a bygone age to keep him occupied for hours. He failed to notice when all the sounds from below ceased and the house settled down into silence, and by the time he realised he was alone the daylight leaking into the attic through cobwebbed skylights was greying into dusk.

Reluctantly, he left the intriguing collection of old clothes, toys, books and household bric-a-brac amongst which he had been rummaging and clattered down three flights of stairs to the hall, only to find that the front door was locked.

* * * * *

Absorbed in these memories, Geraint turns off the street and enters a bar. *It's amazing that I wasn't more scared*, he thinks, as he sips a beer and watches the busy comings and

48

goings around him. Indeed, he does not remember being scared at all. Not, at least, in the beginning.

When he had reached the ground floor with its boarded-up windows it was totally dark. Feeling his way through large and small rooms he tried all the other outside doors. They, too, were locked. He went back upstairs but the windows there were securely fastened, the panes too small to let him out, even if he could have smashed one and risked the terrifying drop to the ground.

Seeing in his mind's eye his own small self, banging on the glass and shouting for help, Geraint orders another beer. *But I didn't panic*, he thinks with some pride. He had been confident that his mother would turn up sooner or later. Or the police!

The dusk, and later the dark, did not trouble him except that they put an end to his explorations. Neither the electricity, the telephone nor (he discovered later) the water was connected in the house. No streetlight glimmered through the trees and the moon when it rose cast little light but created interestingly eerie shadows in the rooms. The worst thing, he remembers, was that he was hungry and thirsty – and very bored. He continued at intervals to bang on the windows and shout until, having elicited no response (for there was no-one within hearing distance), he decided the only thing to do was to sleep. He went back to the turret room favoured by the children and yanking down the heavy curtain he wrapped it round himself and settled on the floor.

He woke at dawn on the following day, and that day had seemed endless. In the course of it he found a flask of cold tea in the kitchen (presumably left by the family when they visited) and in an adjoining pantry a rusty tin of baked beans. This he bodged open with his pocket knife, scooping the beans out one at a time with the same tool.

* * * * *

Geraint has never actually lost the memory of this adventure. But never before has he dwelt on it in such detail. He cannot understand why today he has recalled it with such immediacy that he can smell the tainted air of the house, feel the texture of the velvet curtain against his cheek and hear the erratic creaking of the weather vane. Indeed, he has delved so deeply into it that it is with a shock that he sees that it is already late afternoon of the present day and that the barman is regarding him with a prolonged, puzzled stare.

"You been miles away, mate," the man says suddenly. "It's an hour since you ordered that last pint. Ain't you hungry yet?" He removes Geraint's glass and polishes the bar with a stained cloth. "Can I get you a sandwich?" he asks.

Still half in the past, and suffering the remembered pangs of hunger from fifty years ago, Geraint says, "Thanks. That would be wonderful."

"Ham or cheese?"

"Anything, as long as it's not cold baked beans," says Geraint.

The barman shakes his head and departs. Geraint retreats once more into the past, carried there by the thought that a sandwich offered to him at that time would have been a life-saver – though he cannot recall whether he actually believed he was going to die. At least two days must have passed. He finished the cold tea and could find no more tins of food – or anything else that was edible. He unearthed a battered copy of *Great Expectations* in the attic and read it from cover to cover. He slept when he could.

He grew increasingly bewildered as to why his mother had not found him. As hunger and weakness began to affect him he became afraid that she had abandoned him. Several times he thought or imagined that he heard police sirens in the distance and once even the sound of his own name being shouted through a loudhailer. He banged again and again on the windows and yelled until his dried-out throat seized up . . . but the garden remained as silent and empty as the beginning of the world.

Now, in 2014, sitting in a busy, brightly-lit bar, with an untasted sandwich in front of him, Geraint is assailed by a new and powerful curiosity. His whole life has been driven by the desire to explore, to know, to understand the world in which he lives. His work as a research biologist has depended on it. He has encountered many dangers and discovered many wonders because of it. But what is intriguing and baffling him today is why, in all these years, he has not closely examined this memory before.

"Curiouser and curiouser," he mutters. Because the question which has come to him so belatedly concerns the most curious mystery of all: *why is it that, while every detail of the experience is still vivid and present to him, he cannot remember – cannot reach, even in a momentary flicker of recall – how in the end he had escaped from the house in the wood?*

WINTER BLUES

It began the year that Harriet, suffering from the weather, boredom and a sense of staleness in her marriage, was more than usually afflicted with the winter blues. Because of this she agreed to meet Piers for lunch one day. After a long, intense conversation (tearful on her part, exasperated but then sympathetic on his) he made the suggestion.

"It's time we went further with this," he murmured, leaning across the table and taking her hand in his. His fingers were cool, long and slender.

"Starting next week I'm off on a round of inspections of local offices that will take me all over the county. We could meet regularly for lunch in whatever place I happen to be – it's the perfect opportunity to have secret – and private – assignations . . ."

He raised his dark eyebrows invitingly at her, but Harriet demurred. "I have to be at home for the children coming back from school," she said. "If it's far away I couldn't manage it in time."

Piers smiled.

* * * * *

Over the dark, dreary, waterlogged months that followed, Harriet found herself exploring the county's hidden byways. To her surprise her spirits rose as she drove down twisting lanes while her frantic windscreen wipers struggled to clear the glass. She swished through floods that rose halfway up her tyres, squinted through mist that muffled the line between road and verge and battled with the steering wheel to counter the erratic buffeting of the gales.

With the help of the SatNav Piers had given her, she negotiated unfamiliar market towns and villages, passed through gloomy forests and over moors where huge crags, slick with wet, menaced her through the lowering clouds, and made her way round tricky one-way systems and over bridges beneath which swollen streams churned and frothed.

By some miracle she lost her way only once and mostly she arrived on the stroke of noon at whatever quiet hotel or quaint inn Piers had chosen. Where he had booked a table. And, it turned out, a room.

"But . . !" she protested, the first time. (She had never done anything like this before). "But . . ."

"But nothing!" insisted Piers. "We can have two hours of sheer bliss!"

And so they did. During the first hour there was good food and a small glass of wine for her, a half of beer for him. After that there was a room with wide views of the tumultuous sea, or with latticed windows that faced down a wooded valley, or where the wind howled in the chimney and thrashed the branches of a nearby tree so that it tapped insistently against the glass. Or it might be an attic room perched above an alley where half-timbered houses leaned together like conspirators.

Most often on these days they made love and winced or laughed as the bed creaked and squeaked beneath them. But sometimes, relaxed and lazy after the lunch, they simply lay side by side and talked, discussing ideas, acquainting themselves again with the past or speculating about the future.

* * * * *

As February rained itself out and the days opened up a little to the light, Piers reminded her that their adventure was drawing to its end.

"I've almost finished my tour of inspection," he said. "Next week I have to return to base."

Harriet sat up and stretched. In the mirror over the dressing table she could see her dark blonde hair tousled to curls around her face. Her cheeks, so pale before, were faintly flushed to pink. She realised that the inside clouds had cleared, just as the outside ones had. She felt refreshed, rejuvenated. And she had no regrets over the winter's sneaked pleasures, the stolen afternoons.

Reflected beside her head a brown jug held a dozen early daffodils. She stared at them with an abstracted smile before glancing at her watch. If she was to be home for the children and Piers back on time at the local office, they must leave.

"So, no more time out!" she sighed.

Piers, at the window, finished straightening his tie and turned so that his eyes met hers in the mirror.

"Oh," he said, retrieving his briefcase from the rumpled quilt on the bed. "I don't know about that. After all, every year has its winter . . . "

Harriet laughed.

"What time will you be home tonight, love?" she asked. "If you can make it back before dusk, I think the kids would like to go to the park."

ON THE ALLOTMENT

"No," he had said on that terrible day. "It wasn't me. It was my dog, here. It was Loopy."

The policewoman had smiled and then stooped to stroke Loopy, who was sitting pressed against Harry's leg, one ear raised, brown eyes beseeching in that way dogs' eyes always seemed to do. Beseeching what? he had wondered then. And the girl's eyes had been the same. Beseeching *what*?

Harry winced now at the memory – at the clear, shocking image that for the last six months had kept invading his head, piercing his heart and setting off the same unanswered, unanswerable questions. He unlatched the gate that led into the allotments and hesitated there for a moment before whistling Loopy out of the thicket where she was snuffling and scratching after something. A mouse perhaps, or more likely a rat.

Today was the first time he had come down here since that day, and as he walked slowly along the overgrown path towards his own plot the dog came prancing around him – with pleasure, he supposed, at renewing her acquaintance with this semi-wilderness. Did any flicker of recollection trouble her doggy brain? he wondered. Probably not. She would not have understood the significance of the event they had shared that day. She would just have been doing what lively, friendly and inquisitive dogs do. He envied her.

As he lowered himself on to the rotting wooden bench beside his small sentry-box of a shed he tried not to look down to where the railway ran at the bottom of the allotments. But in spite of himself he found his eyes drawn to the station platform on the far side.

On *that* day its utilitarian glass and steel shelter had been shaded by the trees at the top of the concrete embankment behind it. Ash and sycamore had been lush with new foliage, the birds in their branches competing as to which could sing the loudest. And around him Loopy had been skittish with the excitement of spring.

Today there were few leaves left on the trees and no birds sang.

With an effort Harry wrenched his thoughts away from their obsessive loop about the girl and concentrated on thinking about his wife, Alice. She had been puzzled by his abandonment of the allotment. He had not told her the real reason, unable for once to share something with her. He had merely said there had been an unpleasant incident there.

Knowing that Harry had always treasured the quiet times in his small patch of garden, Alice had been saddened and surprised at his sudden apparently total loss of interest in it, but this morning when she'd asked him to go and pick a winter cabbage for her and he'd shaken his head, she had finally become exasperated.

"What's wrong with you?" she said. "You stubborn old bugger! I *need* a cabbage for Susannah's favourite dish tonight. Remember how she loves sausage and mash with buttered cabbage – *home-grown* buttered cabbage?"

Warmth had filled him at the thought of his precious daughter coming for a rare overnight stay, and with a groan he had relented. But the warmth had drained rapidly away, driven out by the haunting image of the girl again. It had been her resemblance to a younger Susannah that had endowed the event with its peculiarly intense pain.

Appeased by his consent, Alice had said, "– and if you can find any late blackberries there, I'll bake a blackberry-and-apple pie for pudding."

She had helped him on with his coat and run her fingers through his still-abundant hair. "White as swans-down!" she'd murmured. "So why does your beard stay grey as a badger?"

"It's stubborn," he'd said. "Like me! Just give it time."

They had both laughed. Then he had kissed her and left.

He imagined her now, in the neat house only two hundred yards away, indulging in a frenzy of unnecessary housework; scrubbing the kitchen floor or hanging washing on the line in the tiny garden where colour still lingered in her pots of scarlet and pink geraniums. How different from the allotments! Harry let his gaze wander over the whole acre, where – donated by some long-ago benevolent citizen – twenty plots had once flourished, providing fresh vegetables and even flowers for the families who lived in the terraces behind them.

Nowadays entanglements of ivy and Traveller's Joy smothered the derelict sheds and only coarse grass, nettles and docks thrived beneath the brambles and briars that blotted out the boundaries of each plot. A clump of forlorn purple chrysanthemums had managed to survive among some old pea-sticks, a single crimson dahlia drooped inside a stripped runner-bean tripod and, close to the gate, a group of tall, slender stalks still sported a crop of brilliant yellow daisies, but as to the rest, the place was little more than a rubbish dump. Everywhere there was a litter of discarded tools and once useful items: a water-butt here, a rusting bicycle there, a wheelbarrow without its wheel, two plastic garden chairs lying on their sides and a bird-feeder loaded with mouldy peanuts.

After his summer-long absence Harry's own usually tidy plot was not much better. The cabbage he cut for Alice was buried in weeds, but to his surprise was plump and firm, only its outer leaves nibbled to green lace by marauding caterpillars.

As he dusted off the earth and discarded the spoiled leaves, Loopy came flouncing through the undergrowth. He watched her with affection. She was a rescue dog of no known parentage, but her golden coat, floppy ears and foxy muzzle suggested retrievers in her ancestry and, true to form, she now had an ancient, battered tennis ball clamped in her jaws.

"Good girl," he said softly. "A rabbit – or better still a pheasant – might have been more useful, but well done all the same!"

Loopy dropped the ball at his feet and looked up at him with what he always perceived as laughter in her eyes.

Suddenly his breath tightened as he heard the express from Waterloo approaching from the junction half a mile away. For some time he had been aware of the sound of male voices reaching him from the station below and now, without thinking, he glanced down. Five or six lads were larking about in the shelter, but otherwise the platform was deserted. As the train roared out of the short tunnel just up the line the boys, who knew full well it would not stop at this wayside halt, hooted and made rude gestures. Harry clenched Loopy's wrecked ball in his fist and shut his eyes.

What he saw in the darkness behind his closed eyelids was a single solitary figure, teetering on the very edge of the platform, utterly still and silent; an image that had grieved his heart and afflicted his imagination for the last half year.

* * * * *

It had been a weekday morning in early May. There had been no-one else on the allotments and nobody at the station. He and the dog had had the place to themselves. On both sides of the line the trees had been erupting in a slow explosion of green and the air was mellowed by sunlight, spiced with the nutmeg fragrance of the wisteria that scrambled over his small shed. He had been digging his own patch, pausing now and then to straighten his stiffened knees or rub his sore hip. The earth turning under his spade was crumbly and black, well-nurtured over the years, and he remembered feeling happy as he whistled the melody of *Summertime*, one of Alice's favourite songs. Around him Loopy had romped and skittered, chasing shadows.

He recalled that, beneath his joy in the beauty of the morning and the prodigality of the spring, had run an undercurrent of melancholy arising from his awareness of the many uncared-for plots around him.

"Once upon a time," he had said to Loopy, who had stopped for a moment to scratch, "in every plot there would already have been neat rows of plants just showing through the soil, the promise of fresh vegetables to come – each in their own season – for the poor families in the houses up there." He had nodded towards the terraces above them before stooping to dig again.

"And for the men and women who came in their precious hours of free time to work in this quiet place there would have been solace for their hearts and sustenance for their souls".

The dog had given a sharp yap that had sounded to him like derisive laughter.

"I know," he said as he came to the end of the trench. "Old age – and rose-tinted specs!"

It had grown very warm in the sun and, driving his spade into the ground, he had taken off his jacket and gone to place it in the shed. He had picked up the packet of bean seeds he wanted to plant and emerged to the sound of Loopy barking somewhere in the wilderness below him. Wondering what had disturbed her, he called, and when she did not respond he had wandered down the slope to investigate.

It was then that he had first seen, vivid against the grey embankment behind her, the girl in the bright yellow raincoat. The coat was made of some kind of shiny fabric that was designed to repel rain but today reflected back the sun. Its skirt was loose and full, reaching down to her calves. At that point she was pacing up and down the empty platform. Her head, with its tumble of blonde hair (the colour of ripened wheat – so like Susannah's) was bent as if she were watching the movement of her own feet over the grey concrete. Her own *bare* feet . . .

Alerted by the oddness of this (for who would have bare feet in such a place – or wear a raincoat on such a glorious day?), Harry had moved right up to the iron railings that separated the allotments from the railway tracks. Loopy, now silent, leaned against his leg, head raised to him as if to say, "What's going on?"

"Hello, there!" he'd shouted to the girl. "You know there won't be any train stopping here until midday?"

Briefly she had looked up, but without pausing in her walk had raised one hand, delicate fingers spread in a movement that seemed to suggest *Keep away, keep away, please leave me alone* . . .

Even across the space between them he had sensed the distress in her. It was in every line of her body as she continued, head lowered, to pace to and fro, now quickly, now slowly, turning and returning. And although she was entirely alone and he had not spoken again, she kept repeating that gesture with her hand – as if to fend someone off.

By now Harry was alarmed. He knew the London express would pass through the station in five minutes or so. He feared the girl's intention and his mind went into overdrive. Should he call someone? The police? An ambulance? *Anyone?* But what if he were misunder-standing, misinterpreting the situation?

It was then that the girl had stopped walking. She stepped to the very edge of the platform, and in an action so disturbing that it had robbed Harry of breath and imprinted on his mind the image that had tormented him ever since, she had opened her coat wide and holding the two sides up like bizarre yellow wings, had revealed that beneath it she was completely naked.

Her body, young and beautiful and almost as sexless as a child's, was white as milk and painfully thin. While she stood there, motionless, for several seconds, Harry in horror realised three things: that his mobile phone was a hundred yards away in his jacket pocket; that with his arthritic hips and knees, he could not, even in desperation, climb over the head-high, viciously-spiked iron fence that cut him off from her, and that already, in the distance, he could hear the rumble of the approaching express . . .

* * * * *

It seemed that he stood there for hours, immobilised by fear, but in the end it was Loopy who led the way. Just beyond where the platforms ended there was a level crossing for pedestrians. Reached by a narrow lane that wound down beside the allotments, it gave access to the station from the houses on this side of the line and, via the steps up the embankment on the other side, created a short cut to the terraces across the way.

In an agony of anxiety, gasping for breath, Harry followed the dog as she raced to the far end of the allotments. This was the most neglected, most desecrated part of the whole acre and he had to wade through mounds of mouldering plastic bags whose split skins were spilling their filthy contents among other household rubbish tossed down from the houses above. Cursing, he at last arrived where he could see the boarded footway of the crossing.

With an excited yap, Loopy swerved sideways and shot through a gap where the fence had been vandalised, its railings twisted and wrenched apart. Much bulkier than the dog, Harry had had to squeeze himself through, panting and panicky, as he heard the train's siren blare past the junction where the main line joined the local one. By the time he reached the crossing, the train – which had slowed a little over the points – had picked up speed again and was thundering towards the station.

He gritted his teeth against the pain in his joints and pounded across the track. There was nobody else in sight but now he could see the girl again. She had not moved, but stood as still as stone, as if under a spell, her whole being concentrated on watching as the train emerged from the tunnel only a few breaths away.

"No!" he shouted. "Please, please, no!"

But Loopy was before him. No doubt seeing this unusual divergence from the norm as a new game, and attracted as always to people, she flung herself upon the girl who cried out, staggered and (thank God! thank God!) sank to her knees beside the dog while the train, in a stink of diesel fumes and dusty air, passed through.

* * * * *

By the time Harry had reached the girl she was slumped on the flagstones, her arms around an ecstatic Loopy, her face buried in the dog's rough coat and her shoulders shaking with sobs. The yellow mackintosh was wrapped around them both and in an instinctive impulse of modesty she dragged its edges together as he crouched beside them. Lightly, he touched her shoulder, and she looked up at him, her face streaked with tears and her rain-grey eyes anguished. Their expression was beseeching. She did not speak, but once more hid her face against the dog, who nuzzled her dishevelled hair and whined softly, perhaps at the tightness of her grasp.

While Harry had hesitated, longing to comfort the girl and fold her in his arms (but knowing he could not, *should* not), he saw out of the corner of his eye a policewoman begin to descend the steps down the embankment with a man in a uniform he did not recognise (a paramedic or a nurse?) behind her.

They strode towards the group on the platform and, nodding briefly to Harry, took the girl by the arms and raised her from the ground. Loopy, released, stood with her tail wagging and her tongue lolling, while the policewoman gave her a quick pat. He could not tell whether the newcomers had actually witnessed the scene or knew the part the dog had played. Their faces were uncommunicative, as they asked him to describe exactly what *he* had seen, and they seemed to assume that it was he who had saved the girl and averted a tragedy.

"No," he had said. "It wasn't me. It was my dog."

But as they turned away with the unresisting girl between them, he thought that the tragedy, the *real* tragedy, was one that neither he nor Loopy, nor possibly anyone else, could have prevented. It was there in the girl's eyes when she had looked at him: there in the clear expression of her despair as she stood, naked and exposed, on the edge of the platform while the train roared towards her. It was a tragedy that had already happened.

* * * * *

He had dragged himself home that morning, his vision blurred by tears, and had said nothing of the incident to Alice, although he knew she sensed something was amiss. As Loopy, too, seemed aware of his distress, sitting with her head resting on his knee, her eyes begging for a response, he wrestled with the questions he had not been able to ask and that he knew now would never be answered.

In the days that followed he had listened avidly to local news programmes and searched through all the papers. He had found nothing. There was no reference to the incident anywhere. He had even gone to the police station but they had refused all information.

"That's confidential, see, sir," they had insisted politely. They would not even tell him her name.

As the weeks went by and the images receded, reduced in frequency (but never in sharpness) it was not knowing her name that troubled him most. Harry felt this was irrational, even ridiculous. But her namelessness seemed to rob her of her reality, to cancel her out, so that it was as if he had merely dreamed her.

Today, when for the first time he had plucked up the courage to return to the allotments, the unanswered questions roved round his head as he picked the few blackberries he could find for Alice. From the experience of his own happy childhood, his settled and contented present, he could not imagine what it would be like to suffer the powerful forces which had borne down on the girl and driven her to such despair. The possibilities, he knew, were endless: the manifold cruelties of persecution, mental ill health, poverty, sexual abuse, addiction, loneliness, homelessness, abandonment, neglect – and above all, the lack of anyone who really cared . . .

Thinking of these things, Harry felt the world itself was as blighted by lack of care as the allotments around him.

O, I have ta'en too little care of this!

The words of King Lear – the old king's belated realisation that in spite of his wealth and power (or was it perhaps *because* of his wealth and power?) he had failed in what mattered most – in his *humanity* – came, unbidden, into Harry's head.

That was the heart of it, he thought. Nobody who had the *power* to change things – the *means* to rescue the poor, the dispossessed and the nameless – nobody ever **cared** enough . . .

With a sigh he gathered together the cabbage and the half-full container of blackberries, before calling Loopy from her scavenging among the litter for the ball he'd thrown. "Come on, lass," he said. "Let's take these home to Alice."

Loopy gave a quick, staccato bark and raced ahead of him, surging through the patch of bright yellow daisies beside the path, leaving a broken bloom at his feet. Harry stooped with a groan and picked it up. It was exactly the same colour as the girl's raincoat. Sunshine seemed trapped within the flower's petals: the sunshine of the whole summer, retained and then relayed in these dark autumn days.

Harry was not a praying man. He had no confidence in the existence of any god, much less a god who cared individually for the creatures he had brought into being. Today he knew no more of the girl's story than he had on the day her image had etched itself on his memory, and although sunshine had illuminated the image, the memory itself would always be infused with darkness. He knew that for the rest of his life he would remember and grieve for her – and for the fact that he had not been able to help her.

He looked again at the daisy and his footsteps quickened to catch up with Loopy. "But," he said to the dog. "But. *But.* But what if some unknown, unknowable grace should exist *somewhere* in the universe – a grace suggested by the beauty of this flower, by the mystery of life itself – and what if that grace should sometimes . . . *just sometimes,* respond to a desperate human hope?"

Gently he placed the flower on top of the blackberries and opened the gate to let the dog through.

"Oh, if only it could!" he said to Loopy as she brushed past him. "If only my desperate hope could act like the sun on this flower and touch her life with warmth and colour – and love . . . and tenderness . . . and healing . . . and even joy . . ."

Shaking his head, he turned to latch the gate behind him as Loopy, knowing nothing of grief, headed joyfully for home.

"If only!" he said.

THE WRITING ON THE WALL

In all his long life he had never, knowingly, broken the law. He had never challenged authority or society's norms, so when, aged eighty, he first wrote words on a public wall it was therefore a shock to him: a shock composed of mingled horror and delight. He could never, even in his wildest imaginings, have foreseen where that first act would lead.

Having grown up in wartime he remembered the exhortations postered on the walls – *Dig For Victory!* and *Careless Talk Costs Lives!* among them – as well as the usual forbidden words hand-written in chalk. From *these* he had shrunk in embarrassment, not knowing precisely what they meant, but strongly aware of their sexual connections and their ugly intent. Later, in the grim and grimy inner city where he spent most of his adult life, he watched graffiti proliferate: crude artworks that in the course of time were overlaid by others, illiterate scrawls, illegible signatures. It seemed to him that in an already unattractive place they simply added eyesore to eyesore.

Among them real meaning of any kind was scarce, but very occasionally he came across something that amused him, such as

BOYS WILL BE BOYS –
BUT GIRLS WILL BE WOMEN

which he found printed on the wall of the local convent school.

His own first attempt at writing on a wall happened almost by accident. Unable to sleep and plagued by random confused and confusing thoughts, he had risen in the small hours and wandered round his neighbourhood. The streets were quiet and the breaking dawn was laying a grey patina over everything not illuminated by a street-light. As he entered the deeper darkness of a narrow alleyway, where litter spread like an evil fungus, his foot sent something round and metallic rolling away from him. It rattled noisily in the silence and, stooping, he picked it up. By the light of his mobile phone he could see that what he held was a spray-paint canister, and on impulse he pressed the pump.

A jet of white paint arced across the high wall beside him. To his astonishment, a quiver of boyish excitement ran through him and after making a few experimental swirls he started to write:

WHERE LITTER LIES
BEAUTY DIES

The words were not original. He had come across them in a shabby little village in Ireland and they had impressed him with their neat encapsulation of the problem. He slipped the offending can into his pocket, returned home and slept peacefully for the remainder of the night. In the course of the following day an idea that was to transform his life slowly developed.

He became a night prowler. With his spray-can tucked like a gunslinger's weapon in a holster against his hip, he walked the darkest, sleaziest parts of the town, and everywhere he went he left shreds and patches of poetry, dredging up unfinished lines, incomplete stanzas and broken rhythms from the detritus of a lifetime's reading. He scribbled

> ### ENTER THESE ENCHANTED WOODS
> #### YE WHO DARE

on the steel gates of the dingy little local park, and on the sooty churchyard wall he declaimed

> ### THE WORLD IS CHARGED
> #### WITH THE GRANDEUR OF GOD ~
> ### IT WILL FLAME OUT
> #### LIKE SHINING FROM SHOOK FOIL

This was the beginning. Gradually he perfected the art of it. He varied the colours and the type of paint he used, from pastel pale to vibrant and intense. He chose different kinds of lettering to suit the lines, sometimes printing in neat boxy capitals, sometimes letting himself go in a flowing copperplate script, sometimes decorating his initial letters like those he had seen in medieval manuscripts.

In summer he heard the church clocks stutter out three, in winter four, strokes before he retired. He rarely encountered anyone and there was never a policeman in sight. On one hot, dusty night, while involved in a slightly lengthy quotation on the back wall of the town hall, he was joined by a tipsy young man, who stood swaying and muttering, as he watched him write

O western wind when wilt thou blow
That the small rain down can rain ?
Christ, that my love were in my arms
And I in my bed again !

"One of the most perfect poems in the English language, don't you think?" he asked his observer, as he added the final exclamation mark.

"Don't know about tha', mate," the lad responded. "Don't go much for po . . . for pomes meself. But I know wha' tha' bloke means!" Rolling with drink and laughter, he had slouched away into the dark.

From time to time he would go out in the daylight to review his handiwork, and more and more frequently he would find a small group clustered around one of his writings.

"What the hell are *swallowdares*?" someone asked, turning to face the crowd that was puzzling over the words he had written on the florist's wall:

. . . daffodils,
That come before the swallowdares, and take
The winds of March with beauty . . .

A discussion started in which he took no part, but he resolved to be more careful with his spacing in future. It was about the same time that, amidst much dissent, the local bus company decided to change the colours of its vehicles from plain green to purple and yellow. Mischievously, in those same colours, he wrote on the wall of the bus station –

THE ASSYRIAN CAME DOWN
LIKE THE WOLF ON THE FOLD,
AND HIS COHORTS WERE GLEAMING
IN PURPLE AND GOLD

Later that day he strolled down there to see the effect, and heard an elderly bystander exclaim, "It's high time someone caught this blighter! He's making a laughing-stock of the town."

But he was not caught. The police were convinced the perpetrator must be young and put extra pressure on the local gangs, who understandably reacted with outrage at being suspected of such nerdy stuff. The press dubbed him 'The Ghost Writer of Grimestown' and published pages of speculation before getting bored and abandoning the story. The Book Group at the library set up a competition to trace the origins and authorship of the poems, while the Youth Club (much run-down but energised by the challenge) tried to work out whether some sort of rebellious, subversive message were being transmitted in code.

Gradually, however, what he had begun to hope would happen, did happen. Other people began to add their own favourite lines. They ranged from the lyrical

> *That's the wise thrush; he sings each song twice over,*
> *Lest you should think he never could recapture*
> *That first fine careless rapture!*

through the elegiac

> REMEMBER ME WHEN I AM GONE AWAY,
> GONE FAR AWAY INTO THE SILENT LAND

the mysterious

> Then look for me by moonlight,
> Watch for me by moonlight
> I'll come to thee by moonlight,
> though hell should bar the way

and the possibly threatening

BEWARE! BEWARE!

HIS FLASHING EYES, HIS FLOATING HAIR!

to the boldly dramatic or foreboding

IT WILL HAVE BLOOD, THEY SAY.

BLOOD WILL HAVE BLOOD.

The extracts were as short as half a line or as long as several stanzas. The ugly town, once wholly prosaic, was in thrall to poetry. It grew beautiful with thoughts and observations expressed in the most marvellous way of which language is capable. Litter disappeared from the hidden corners where people now gathered to read the latest additions. Walls, filthy with the accretions of years, were cleaned, even whitewashed, to give better visibility to the words that bloomed on them. Other languages joined in. The attention of a wider world was caught and the infection spread. His writing on the wall went viral.

By now he was ninety years old and the night ramblings were wearying him. Besides, so many others had taken up the task that in his own town it was becoming difficult to find wall space. He decided it was time to retire.

For so many years he had been a poor sleeper, but now at last he slept untroubled by agitating thoughts or dreams

– but with poetry beating steadily in his blood like a strong, quiet pulse.

WHEN THE WINDS BLOW

It is when the wind blows that she sees him, but only when it blows from the south – which in this bleak land is rare. It is for this reason she loves the south wind. This, and the fact that it carries a faint, Mediterranean warmth on its breath. Perhaps it is only in her imagination, but she feels that she can even catch the scent of herbs as the breeze wafts in through her open window. Rosemary, oregano, thyme . . .

Ah, time! How long ago it all was! He would be almost an old man by now. That is something she cannot imagine although she tries. She often tries – but his face always evades her. It is only when this gentle wind blows that she sees him clearly, and then it is as a child, as he was on *that* day, the day when he first confronted – and conquered – fear.

Perched in the branches of the ancient apple tree whose outermost twigs still brush her walls, he sits astride a bough. He turns to smile at her. It is a smile of triumph because he has at last climbed high, as high as the sturdiest branches will allow. The south wind shivers the new leaves and ruffles the dark blond curls that reach to his shoulders – curls that he would like shorn, but that she cannot bear to lose. His blue eyes seem to reflect the sky, a soft forget-me-not-blue.

The bough sways in a stronger gust and he clutches at it, his knuckles whitening against the grey bark. But he does not change his position except to turn his head and look away from her. She sees his clear, childish profile, his long lashes fluttering

with the nervous blinking of his eyes as he stares out at the view.
She knows that, from where he sits, he can see across the garden
to the water meadows beyond, where the cattle browse again after
the long winter. In the middle distance the river will be glinting
like an uncoiling ribbon sprinkled with Christmas glitter. And
at the far horizon he will be able to see the shimmer and shine of
the sea . . .

She sighs as a small island of cloud floats across the sun
and the world darkens. The vision has gone: the tree is
empty.

On the day he went away, pausing for only a second to
look back, it had been a very different wind that blew. It
had come roaring in from the north-east, cold with the first
hint of winter, rough and harsh as it tossed the apple tree
until the boughs groaned and the last of the unpicked
apples tumbled to the ground.

He had straightened his shoulders and clutched his cap
as the wind snatched at it. He had been tall, then, and long-
limbed, with an easy, loping stride. The open, direct gaze
of his blue eyes revealed so much about him – his honesty,
his kindliness, the curiosity in him that embraced all
things. Hidden in their depths where only she could see it
was his vulnerability, his fear. He had waved to her and
smiled before turning away to set off whistling down the
road that led to the sea.

When the wind blows from the north and the east she does not *see* him.   But she remembers.   She remembers how he went with the first dead leaves of autumn and the dust of the long summer swirling round his feet. She remembers how they all went, and how the bitter wind blew him and most of his generation away in a tempest that shook the whole world and from which, she thinks, it has not, even yet, recovered . . .

VÉRONIQUE

As he sorted through his collection of black and white photographs the portrait slid from between two Breton landscapes and fell to the floor. Creakily he stooped to retrieve it.

Véronique!

Unusually for him nowadays, the name came immediately. He adjusted his spectacles, gazed into the timeworn face and was transported straight back to the long-ago, far-away morning when he had encountered her: to the stony farm track, the grey dawn light, the mingled smells of manure and newly-mown hay and the husky rasp of her aged voice . . .

He and his wife had rented a small cottage in a remote, forgotten village in the heart of Brittany. It had been at a time when, preparing for retirement, he had taken up photography as a hobby and every morning, long before anyone else was stirring, he had set off with his camera to explore the surrounding area. He had wandered the quiet lanes, taking pictures of tumbledown houses, derelict barns, hedgerows wreathed with dog roses, cattle up to their knees in mist. He rarely saw another person, except for the occasional man who might be a farm worker, perhaps, who nodded in response to his polite *"Bonjour, monsieur,"* before moving on.

The old woman in the photograph had startled him by suddenly looming up over the top of a hedge and flapping a duster right in his face. She, too, had been startled but as he stuttered greetings and apologies to her in his schoolboy French, she had pushed her way through a gap between the hedge and a rickety fence to stand, arms akimbo, in the road before him.

Immediately a torrent of guttural Breton French had swept over him and, confused and uncertain, he had wondered if she were angry at his intrusion. Behind her he could see a tiny cottage: dilapidated blue shutters nearly bare of paint flanked the single window; hollyhocks, their flowers touched to crimson and dusky pink by the rising sun, stood against the stone wall, and a ginger cat strolled out of the open doorway, stretched and then settled down on the path to groom itself. From somewhere close by he had been able to hear the cackle of hens.

Now as he studied the portrait, trying to judge its merit as a photograph, these memories returned to him in a tangled mixture of sensations, striking him with a force and intensity that surprised and unsettled him.

The woman, he remembered, had suddenly stopped speaking and pointed to the camera slung around his neck. He had tried to explain his interest in photography, his admiration for her landscape, and she had laughed, indicating that what she wanted was his name. He had given it.

"*Et vous, madame?*" he asked.

"*Véronique,*" she had said.

Slowly a stumbling conversation had begun.

Trying to summon up details, he closed his eyes. He could recollect little of what they had said but could still see the woman as clearly as if her image had been printed on his brain.

She was large, nearly as tall as himself and clad in layers of ill-matching clothes that bulked her out still further. The dress she wore, which looked black in the photograph, had been a dark red, the old-fashioned pinafore on top of it faded to a dirty white.

Her deeply creviced face, her eyes (he could not recall their colour, only that they glinted with amusement), her mobile mouth, her hair dragged back beneath a narrow band and looking as though it had been chopped with garden shears, all mesmerised him. An old peasant woman, he thought, of a kind almost extinct even then. Of the earth, earthy. Rooted in the local soil, the local culture. Marked by lifelong hardship and poverty. But his photograph revealed her exactly as he remembered her – still very much alive – and vibrant with the energy of a powerful personality.

He had asked if she had lived all her life in the village. No, she said. She had spent the war years in Paris.

"*Qu'est-ce que vous avez fait comme travail*? What work did you do?" he had asked.

She laughed again and looked coy. "*J'étais putain*," she said.

He had shaken his head, not knowing what the word meant and she had giggled, done a little seductive shuffle in her ragged slippers and repeated, *"J'etais putain, monsieur. Prostituée!"*

The astonishment, possibly embarrassment, he had felt clearly showed in his face and she had pretended to wipe tears from her eyes.

"Vous n'y croyez pas! You do not believe it!" she said. *"Mais à cette époque j'étais belle, monsieur –* in those days I was beautiful."

Gallantly he had asserted, *"*M*ais vous êtes toujours belle, madame –* you are beautiful now!"

It was then that he had persuaded her to let him take her photograph. Entirely without self-consciousness, she had looked him directly in the eye and smiled for him.

Looking at the image thirty years later, when he himself was creased and crooked with age, he felt he had spoken nothing but the truth.

Véronique had indeed been beautiful!

THE REUNION

The Reunion *is loosely based on a traditional fairy story.*
The clues as to which story it is are in the text.

I   SIMON

The cottage was comfortless. Instead of the brightness I remembered there was gloom – a darkness exaggerated by the heavy clouds massing across the sky. I wandered out of the kitchen and into the old sitting room. Nothing had materially altered: even the furniture was the same, shabbier but unchanged. Back in the kitchen I noted that the old curtains, white muslin sprigged with pink rose-buds, were still at the windows. How we teased Gwyn about those! Such romantic, old-fashioned tastes, we said. But they were dingy now, the hems fraying and the whiteness greyed by the dirt of decades.

Ten minutes later there was still no sign of Graham. I ran my finger across the scarred wood of the kitchen table. Dust rose and slowly settled again. Blast! That would set me off! In the window there was a dead geranium, its leaves brown and crisp.

What's brown and crisp and dangles from the ceiling?
An Irish electrician. Boom! Boom!

Oh, those daft, innocent, politically incorrect jokes we used to share! I started to sneeze, as I knew I would, digging in my pocket for a handkerchief that was not there.

"Good God! Are you *still* sneezing?" The voice came from the open door. "I'd know those explosions any-where. Always drove me mad, your nasal incontinence."

Graham. At last. He strutted across the room (same old G, then) and offered me his hand.

"How's things?" he asked, but without waiting for an answer he turned away and surveyed the room. "Hell's teeth," he said. "The place looks terrible. D'you suppose it's been cleaned since David bought it? Or even since we all left?"

Thirty years, I thought. How can it be thirty years? Time had fattened him, darkened his once fair skin and stolen most of his hair, but his voice, always rather lugubrious, was the same. Fastidiously he flicked dust off the lapel of his smart suit. I sneezed again, several times. From long-ago habit I crossed to the dresser and opened the drawer where Gwyn used to put handkerchiefs, white as snow and neatly ironed, but there was nothing there except mouldy crumbs and a rag of old duster. I glanced at Graham, saw he was staring out of the window, and hastily blew my nose on the duster before stashing it in my pocket.

"Miserable day out there," he said. "Wife all right, is she? Your job OK? Still teaching at the same school?"

I nodded, tried to remember his present marital status, knowing he had divorced Jane years ago . . . It was so long since we'd had any contact. Even cards at Christmas.

"Amazing, really," I said, giving up the attempt to remember, "David managing to track us both down."

"Dozy beggar," he said, taking off his spectacles and polishing them on a pristine handkerchief. "What's he ever made of his life? Drifting from one place to another, full of arty-farty notions, buying this place and then leaving it to rot! I reckon he's kept it as a shrine. To Gwyn. To his youth . . ."

"To all our youths," I said.

Graham glowered at me over his spectacles and uneasily I wondered how we had ever been so close, such friends. At least with David I could still see how . . .

"Actually, he's doing rather well as a photographer," I said.

"What!? Weddings? Corporate get-togethers? Civic occasions?"

"No. Not that. Art photography. He had an exhibition in London in the spring."

Graham's full lips turned down. "So what about these photographs he's put together, the ones he's summoned us all here to see? Just snapshots surely – faded snaps of the four – of the *five* of us . . . nothing *naughty* I hope . . ."

He gave a short, humourless laugh and looked at his watch.

No, I thought, there would be nothing 'naughty'. I was sure of that. David had been a romantic and a dreamer, and he had worshipped Gwyn. But I wondered about Graham. He had claimed to be in love with her, and being competitive by nature he would have had to compete.

Also, in his terms her beauty would have made her a prize catch. She was not really his type, however: too unsophisticated . . .

"Where the hell *is* David?" he grumbled. "I have to be back in Brum for a meeting at two."

"He's upstairs," I said. "Snoozing."

"Sneezing! Not him, too?"

"No, idiot!" (How oddly one falls back into adolescent speak!) "He's sleeping. Been up most of the night apparently, finishing off the album."

There was a hefty thump on the ceiling above us and we both glanced up.

"Fallen out of bed?" For the first time I caught a hint of warmth or amusement in Graham's voice. "Better call him down, Simon. He'll be snail-slow, anyway."

"Still an old grouch, I see!" David's lightly drawled words reached us before he did. He stooped under the stairs door, tall and lanky as ever, raggedly cropped grey hair flopping over his eyes, his face above the full beard crinkling into a smile. Under his arm was tucked a large, silver-backed photograph album. Dusting the tabletop with his sweater sleeve, he put it down before offering his hand to Graham. "Good to see you, mate," he said.

"Could have saved yourself a lot of bother," said Graham, looking down at the book. "Could have done this electronically."

"I could. But I didn't want to."

David urged us to sit down.   As we did so the dust rose again and I sneezed. Graham sighed. With slow, ceremonial care, David opened the album.

II DAVID

Strange how people change utterly over the years – yet do not change at all. I wouldn't have recognised either of these two had I met them in the street, but here, in this context, they seem as familiar as brothers: Simon still sneezing, Graham still grumpy!

The first photograph in the album – black and white, of course – was taken of them both here in the kitchen with Gwyneira, the day she moved in. The shock of that! The surprise and delight – followed by the uncertainty as to what we should do. A girl! When we had expected a boy. Gwyn, she'd signed herself when she applied for the room here. A boy's name, we had thought, and her strong masculine handwriting had given us no reason to doubt. In fact I remember our only doubts were to do with the Welsh bit! We'd assumed (correctly as it turned out) that the applicant was Welsh, and Graham had a thing about the Welsh . . .

But oh, that lovely lilt! Those precisely enunciated consonants!

"Get on with it, man," said Graham, breaking into my thoughts. "We haven't got all day . . ."

"Stunning," murmured Simon, leaning closer over the picture. "Look at that floss of black hair against her creamy skin!"

"And remember those cornflower-blue eyes!"

"Her strength. Her gentleness . . ."

"Her wonderful, strict, old-fashioned housekeeping!"

Simon glanced around the untidy room and blew his nose on what looked to me like a scrap of old duster.

"I know. The place is a mess." I could hear the defensive note in my own voice. "But I only use it as a bolt-hole. I intend to make it more homelike when I retire and live here full time. You realise no-one has lived here since we were here? It's been empty all this time."

"What in God's name do *you* need a bolt hole for?" Graham sounded sour. *"You've* no wife to escape from!"

"You bloody old misogynist," said Simon. Then, turning to face me, he asked if I had bought the cottage in memory of Gwyn. He was always the shrewd one – which surprised me in someone who could seem a bit staid. But he was the kindest of us all . . .

"Not really," I said. (Oh, equivocation!) "I just happened to see it advertised in the local rag and came to look. I remembered, of course. How could I not? The good times. Her. Us. But mainly it was that I felt totally at home here . . ."

(And why did I feel so at home? Because the brief years here were the happiest of my life. I had lived them under an enchantment.)

Graham was turning the pages. Too fast. The pictures flicked by like scenes in a magic-lantern show: pictures of all of us absorbed in our books, studying around this table under the lamp she'd shaded with her shawl; Graham out in the lane, posing on his new bike; Simon and Gwyn all dressed up for tennis; me, sprawled in the old hammock, fiddling with the camera . . .

(What was it? An Olympus? There were fewer pictures of me, anyway: I was always the photographer . . .)

"Not sure I want to do this," said Graham suddenly. "Don't believe in going back into the past. Not sure she'll want to either . . ."

"Course she will. After all, it's a story with a happy ending." Simon sounded brisk. "And the pics are great, David. Don't know what you've done with them, but they're as fresh as yesterday! It was a splendid idea to do this for their wedding . . ."

(I was disconcerted by the sudden chill around my heart. Had I really still hoped she might one day . . . ?)

"Ah!" said Graham, pausing in turning the pages. "There he is. Prince Charming himself. The dream lover for whom she held us all at arm's length – even before he actually arrived in the flesh!"

"And what an arrival! Head first off that crazy old motorbike of his and straight over the hedge –"

"Landing – quite literally – at her feet . . ."

"Astonishing he didn't break that classically chiselled nose of his!"

Graham pushed the album aside, stood up and began pacing the kitchen. He flung open cupboard doors and peered inside. "You haven't got a drink lurking anywhere in this godforsaken place, have you?"

Before I could answer, Simon leapt up and made for the door. "I've a shot or two of whisky in the car," he said.

"No glasses," I warned. "Cups in the sink will have to do."

"Bloody hell, David!"

Graham slumped back onto his chair and we both looked again at the picture of Gwyn and Prys, arms around each other, laughing, young, beautiful . . .

"It had to be because he was Welsh," said Graham.

"Nonsense!" Simon bounced back in, brandishing a half-empty bottle. He crossed to the sink and sloshed water into three chipped cups, dried them on a corner of the curtain and then poured three large whiskies. "It was love at first sight," he said. "Love for life. Love as we'd all wish it to be."

Graham snorted into his drink and then downed it in one.

III   GRAHAM

Bloody Simon! Unreconstructed romantic! Bad as each other, he and David. Never grown up. I was desperate to bring things to a close before they got totally maudlin. I could already feel the melancholy closing in on us . . . not much helped by the liquor either. Cheap stuff, of course. Simon stuck in a second-rate teaching job and can't afford better, I suppose.

When they were both well into their nostalgic, highly-coloured reminiscences, I pointed out that Gwyneira had been the principal author of her own misfortunes.

"Should have known better," I said. "It wasn't the dark ages! Most of us by then were well wised up on how not to get into that sort of trouble."

They were staring at me, David's dark eyes brooding and Simon's red from dust-induced watering – or maybe, for heaven's sake, with unshed *tears*.

"Well, some of the reactions, as well as the awful consequences," said Simon, "*were* out of the dark ages! Gwyn being expelled from the university – and that petty power-in-the-land, his Neanderthal father, taking Prys away and sending him to the States to finish his education!"

He flushed with retrospective anger. Made him look better. He is still a good-looking guy, even now, except for his complexion. That has always tended to the sallow. Still has his hair though, lucky beggar, and scarcely grey yet, either.   Or perhaps, being blonde, it was hard to see . . . Always thought it was him she'd end up with . . .

David closed the album.   Perhaps he could not bear to see that particular picture. Both of them so clearly in love, so ecstatic. I remembered how *he* had been dotty about her. But he was such a Dopey-Joe! Too slow even to see where things were going after Prys turned up . . .

"It meant their best years were lost," said Simon. "But at least they . . ."

Tired, and irritated by all this sentiment, I cut him short.

"There's little point in them marrying now, as far as I can see. Too late for children. Only old age to look forward to . . . "

"I don't think so," David said quietly. "Anyway, they have a child! Don't you remember, Gray? In spite of all the opposition, Gwyn refused to give her up. She went travelling with the baby.   Took the hippy trail through India, Thailand, the Far East . . ."

He paused, sipped daintily at his drink, like a woman. "How brave was that?"

"And how like Gwyneira!" Simon said.

The room had grown suddenly darker and, looking up, I saw the first splotches of rain like scattered stars on the window. Hell, I thought. I've left my umbrella in the car!

"Don't suppose you have a brolly here?" I asked. "It's about to tip it down and I really do have to go."

Neither of them answered me, so I went in search of one, and as I left the room I heard Simon say, "Is there a photo of the child in the album?" I didn't hear David's reply, but five minutes later when I came back they were talking about Gwyn and Prys's daughter.

"I haven't seen her since she was about ten or eleven," said Simon. "When she and Gwyneira went to Canada. Apparently it was she who brought them together again. After the death of her stepfather out there they came back to England, and not unnaturally the girl wanted to meet her real father."

"What about Prys?" I asked. "Where was he? Was he still *single*? Can't imagine it!"

"London," said Simon, shortly, "and divorced."

Clearly he was displeased with me. It reminded me of how he would sometimes sulk after a quarrel. But then he asked me if I had found an umbrella and when I said no, he took his anorak off the back of his chair and offered it to me with a smile. By this time the rain was pelting down. Muddy trails snaked across the filthy window and great gouts of water splashed onto the sill from the broken gutter above.

Without warning I was swept by a surge of confused and confusing emotions – sorrow for the cottage that had been so cared for, so pretty (yes, pretty!) when she was in charge and was now so neglected, dilapidated and sad; gladness, for Gwyneira and her prince whose romance had

114

been so powerful, whose dreams had been shattered but who now, against all the odds were going to be together, and affection for these two aging, failing men whose days here, like mine, had been warmed and made memorable by her . . .

"Will you be coming to the wedding?"

It was David who spoke and to my own surprise – and quite contrary to my original intention – I heard myself say, "Wouldn't miss it for the world."

He grinned his old, slow, boyish grin. "And you're happy with our gift to them? With the album?"

"It's perfect," I said.

"See you then," said Simon. "Leave my anorak somewhere under a bush before you get into the car, will you?"

I stepped out into the wet. A break in the clouds let through a gleam of sunlight and in the haze over the distant hills I could just discern the arc of a rainbow. Looking back I saw Simon's and David's faces, pressed like children's against the grimy, rain-blurred window. They were both smiling, and for the first time in years, it seemed to me, I felt a lightness round my heart.

Raising my hand in farewell, I smiled back.

ANGEL WITH GREEN WINGS

The boyhood exploits of my great-grandfather, Elfyn Parry, are the stuff of family legend. I do not remember him, of course, only the stories about him which were passed down to me. I also have a photograph which shows him to have been a slight, wiry man with dark raggedly curly hair. Although the picture is faded now, his dark eyes still reflect the light in a way that seems to give them a per-manent wicked twinkle – and his ears are pointed!

"He spoke fluent Welsh," my father told me. "Not common in the northern Marches. When annoyed, he would come out with peppery outbursts that sounded totally outlandish to his listeners!"

I guess that all this, together with his name, made Elfyn seem like some kind of changeling, a mischievous sprite from another world. His boyhood mischief, however, was fairly innocent and even in his late teens when he became the leader of a local gang his pranks were inventive and witty rather than wicked.

On one occasion, for instance, the young men carried the car of the aggressively English vicar up to the top of Cynfach Mountain (no roads up there in those days) and left it perched on the summit with the red Welsh dragon flying from its bonnet. On another they sneaked down late one night to the White Lion pub where they unhitched a pony and trap left in the yard by a farmer with whom they frequently crossed swords. Knowing he would be staggering-drunk by the time he emerged, they led the pony out through the gate, which they latched shut before reharnessing the pony to the trap on the inside. Then they waited for the fun to start. It was all harmless enough stuff, as I said.

There is one story, however, of an exploit that was not so innocuous.

In the days of my great-grandfather's youth every village seemed to have in its population a character who was slightly 'simple' – someone considered to be 'not quite right in the head' – who was sometimes (sadly) referred to as 'the village idiot.' In Cynfach it was Dafi Benyon. Large, lumbering, drooling and unable to speak clearly, he was treated kindly on the whole, though teased and sometimes cruelly imitated by other boys of his own age.

One day when my great-grandfather and his friends were larking about under the churchyard wall, Dafi came stumbling and gesticulating through the lych-gate. Incoherent with excitement, he made them understand he wanted to show them something in the graveyard. Then he led them to a statue newly erected over a child's grave. It was a marble angel as tall as a man, one hand posed coyly on its breast, the other pointing heavenwards. Its freshly polished white stone glittered in the sun.

"Ook . . . ook," stuttered Dafi. "Anjoo . . . iv gyeen . . . gereen . . . wins!"

"What's he saying, the daft bugger?" asked one boy. "Or is he speaking Welsh?"

Elfyn shook his head. "Come on, Dafi," he said, gently enough. "Slow down. Say it again *slowly*."

"*Anjoo* . . . iv . . . gyeen . . . *ings*," repeated Dafi obediently.

There was a short silence and then laughter, and since there was not much fun to be had out of this, the other boys soon drifted away. But over the next few weeks my great-grandfather discovered that Dafi was obsessed by the angel and that he spent hours sitting on the tomb among the wilting flowers, humming and muttering to himself.

"What's so fascinating about that angel, Dafi?" he asked. "Does it *talk* to you?"

Dafi looked at Elfyn with a flicker of scorn in his blue eyes.

"Silly!" he shouted. "Ook! . . . *Green* . . . *wings*!"

My great-grandfather looked in bewilderment at the angel's swan-white wings, but failed to see that the sunlight, shining through the leaves of an overhanging tree, was shedding a faint green radiance across them.

"Dafi Benyon's getting madder by the day," Elfyn said later to his friends. "He spends all his time mooning about around little Bronwen Pugh's grave and believes the lardy-looking angel on it has *green* wings!"

As they were all laughing about this, the idea for a new escapade was born. Elfyn was sent off to his father's workshop to fetch some old dustsheets and while there he also unearthed, from among the clutter on his father's bench, a tin of bright green paint. He used this to colour the cloths and later, with the help of the other boys, he constructed a frame on which they stretched the cloth to make a pair of large, kite-like wings. The next day they all rose early and, carrying the ungainly wings between them, went down to the churchyard. Here they strapped the wings firmly to the angel before concealing themselves behind various gravestones and waiting for Dafi to arrive.

A blustery wind had got up and when Dafi came singing and stuttering into the churchyard it was thrashing the branches of the tree above the grave. Beneath them the green wings suddenly filled like sails, flailing and flapping and beating against the air as if the angel were desperately trying to rise from its plinth. The noise was tremendous. Dafi gave a shocked and terrified cry and ran wildly around the graves before rushing out into the street. The watching boys were hysterical with laughter until, from the road, they heard the squeal of car brakes and another quite different kind of cry, followed by long moments of total silence.

Horrified, Elfyn led the others back out under the lych gate. There was Dafi, sprawled in the road, one leg twisted beneath him, his head bleeding and his face contorted with pain. The car that had hit him was skewed across the lane and its driver was bending over Dafi, who was now moaning softly.

"He came out of there like a bat from hell," said the man, white-faced. "Go and fetch a doctor, will you?"

Dafi survived, but a crippling limp in his damaged leg became yet another burden he had to bear. My great-grandfather had his own burden, of course, and for the rest of his life was racked by guilt and remorse.

"And though he kept his mischievous twinkle," said my father, "it was the end of his *actual* mischief. My own memory of him is that he was an exceptionally kind man, generous and unfailingly thoughtful to others . . . and especially to Dafi himself."

There is a strange little coda to this story.

Years later my great-grandfather surprised his friends and family by telling them that, one limpid April morning when he was on his way to work, he saw an angel. It was, he swore, stooping over Dafi's cottage where, unknown to Elfyn, the now elderly Dafi had just passed away.

He told them that the angel's wings were tipped with green and showed clearly against the pale sky, where it hovered for some moments, its feathers fluttering in the dawn breeze. Then, slowly and silently, it floated up from the valley and drifted over the mountain. The old man apparently always maintained that flashes of green lightning played around it as it disappeared into the clouds, while drops of rain, shining like emeralds, scattered over Dafi's roof.

MARIA TYRGU

The name was lodged in Victor's brain like a burning fragment of shrapnel. Over the years it had seared its way through a wider and wider swathe of his consciousness – and his conscience – until it had driven him in old age to undertake the long and difficult journey he was about to make.

"I have to go," he told his protesting wife, "before it is too late."

"It's probably too late already," she said. "The man you're looking for may well die before you reach him. And you have lived with this uncertainty for so long that surely you can endure it for whatever time you have left – which cannot be much!"

"The older I get, the worse it grows," said Victor. "More and more insistently it returns to me in dreams as well as in daytime flashbacks. That row of kneeling girls!" He shuddered. "What I did! It was terrible . . . *inhuman!*"

"Terrible, certainly," said his wife. "But it was all *too* human!" Asperity gave her usually soft voice a harsh edge. "It was *war*, for heaven's sake. A commonplace of war!"

Victor slid a wad of documents into his case and shrugged on his overcoat.

"Yes," he agreed, as he kissed her goodbye. "It *was* war. But I was the one who committed the atrocity: I, and I alone. What's more, I betrayed *myself*, for I had always

thought of myself as a just man. And it is the *injustice* of
what I did that haunts me . . ."

* * * * *

Later, as the trains carried him across the endless plains
of a continent, through forests and mountains, past the
industrial backsides of restored and thriving cities, he
contemplated again and again, that long row of kneeling
girls . . .

Behind them he saw the ruined village, its stones
blackened by fire, its trees scorched, its roofs collapsed. A
thin March wind stirred the tattered remains of a curtain at
a shattered window. It ruffled the girls' rags and cut
through his greatcoat so that his flesh shrank.

For hours he had been patient while the women were
interrogated, bullied, and finally tortured.

*Which one? Which one of you gave succour to the enemy
airman? Assisted his escape?*

Silence, except for the occasional whimper. The girls,
all cousins, friends or neighbours, reacted according to
their individual personalities, but none had confessed to
knowledge or guilt. The tallest, the one they called Maria
Tyrgu, had stayed stone-faced and silent throughout.

Now, as he watched them shivering from cold and fear,
out of the corner of his eye he saw the white cat emerge
mewling from a nearby barn. He heard the shot fired by

one of his men and saw the girls jump and wince as the cat leapt and dropped on to the cobbles, a mangled scrap of bloodied fur.

Every girl in the kneeling row lowered her head still further, dark and light heads drooping, eyes hidden. Only Maria Tyrgu looked up. Her eyes, a piercing blue, met his, anger and accusation flaring in them.

"There is no evidence," she said, her voice clear and precise. "You have no evidence."

Unable to hold her gaze, he had glanced away to where his men stood leaning on their rifles, chatting and smoking. Time was running out. It was imperative they move on. Maria's defiance and the women's blank female obstinacy frustrated and infuriated him.

As always when he relived this scene, Victor remembered how, with a sickening mixture of disgust and pleasure, he had imagined giving the order to fire. In his mind's eye he had seen the men snapping to attention, lining up, raking the girls with gunfire, reducing them to broken dolls.

When he turned back to face the kneeling row, Maria Tyrgu's head was still raised. Bold, brazen and challenging, she had looked at him with contempt as if she could read his thoughts. That was the moment he made the decision. Withdrawing his pistol from its holder, he had stepped swiftly across the space between them, set the barrel to her temple and pressed the trigger.

129

He had had no evidence against her.

He let the others go: watched them scramble to their feet and stumble away; waited motionless as they fled across the fields to find whatever shelter they could.

* * * * *

Through all the long years since then, Victor had searched for the one person who might absolve him. Hundreds of letters, telephone calls and emails had been sent and received. From the beginning he had realised that the airman he sought was almost certainly long dead. Injured in the crash, alone in enemy occupied territory, penniless and friendless, how could he have survived? All the agencies Victor contacted had told him so. His friends and family and his long-suffering wife had told him so. Moreover, like Victor himself, the man would now have reached an age when still to be alive was unlikely.

But in this case, too, there was no evidence. The man *could* still be alive. So Victor, driven by a need that grew greater as the years went by, persisted. It had taken courage and tenacity, a tenacity he felt he owed to the girls who had knelt in that long row in a shared determination to be silent. Above all, he owed it to Maria Tyrgu . . .

* * * * *

Now, at last, his tenacity rewarded, he stood in another silence.

Face to face with a withered stranger in a strange land, he asked the question he had come to ask. The man, bearded and grey-haired, leaned on his stick and looked at him out of blurred blue eyes.

"*Maria Tyrgu?*" he said, repeating the name that Victor had spoken.

"After your plane came down," prompted Victor, "a girl in the village saved your life. Aided your escape. Was her name Maria Tyrgu? Or –" he spoke with a tremor, suddenly fearful "– or was it some other girl? Some other name? Given the circumstances, surely you must recall?"

The old man stared into the distance, a frown of concentration drawing his frayed eyebrows together.

"No," he said slowly, at last. "The name means nothing to me. How could it be otherwise? One girl out of dozens who helped me? It has gone. Disappeared. Been extinguished by time. I'm sorry – but I simply cannot remember!"

INHERITANCE

I THE BOOKS

I suppose this story really begins with my grandfather, Henry Grey, but after his death it went underground before beginning again, three months before I was born, with the death of his son, my father, Henry Llewelyn Grey.

So let us say this story begins with my father. More accurately, it both begins and ends with him. Yet until recently I knew only the barest facts of his life.

He was born in 1910 in the Border Marches of North Wales (not far from where I myself now live). To me his boyhood is a blank, but I know that by the thirties he was working abroad as a civil engineer. Early in 1939, with war threatening, his firm brought him back to supervise the construction of a local factory where Wellington bombers were being built. Because this work was considered essential to the war effort he was not called up and it was while he was there that he met and married my mother. They rented a small house in Bryn Afon until, with the work on the factory completed, he was sent to another job at John Brown's shipyard in Glasgow.

My mother stayed in Bryn Afon. She did not want to give up her secretarial post at the aircraft factory and, knowing there could be further moves, she opted not to go to Scotland with my father. Then, very late in the war, with the work on the dockyard finished, my father was unexpectedly conscripted into the army.

Thus in 1945, when most of our troops were returning from Europe, he was posted over there to help clear up the mess created by our bombers. With his unit of the Royal Engineers he was demolishing a bridge that had collapsed into the River Meuse when he was gravely injured. He spent some months in hospital in Fumay before being sent home, where he survived for only one year. That was the year in which I, Louis Llewelyn Grey, was conceived.

Before he died my father knew I was on the way and apparently expressed a wish that if I were a boy I should be named Louis.

"I believe," my mother said, "that Louis was the name of the doctor who treated him in Fumay."

She did not say then, or ever, that my father had not wanted me to have a name that derived from my grandfather, but from what I have recently discovered, I suspect that this was his true motivation for breaking with family tradition. My mother rarely spoke to me about my father although once, in a confiding moment, she said that I had inherited my blonde hair (which is still plentiful but with age has faded to the colour of dust) and my blue eyes from him. She also maintained that I owe my quirky sense of humour and my quick temper to Henry Llewelyn.

Looking back, I feel I must have been a peculiarly incurious child, as I never asked her for more information – something that strikes me now as strange and sad.

The only other inheritance I had from him (and this I shared with my mother) was his collection of books. These consisted mainly of heavy tomes of information on the history and practice of civil engineering, but they included a score or so of classic novels and two anthologies of poetry. From my childhood I was an avid reader and these books were the beginnings of an education that led eventually to my becoming a teacher of literature. So a love of books, I guess, is another of his legacies to me.

From as far back as I can remember, my mother struggled to make ends meet, frequently moving house either to reduce costs or to be closer to a job with better prospects. But my father's books always came with us. When I was twelve she remarried and life became more settled. My stepfather was a decent man. He brought me up well and kindly but there were no children of this marriage and after he died my mother came to live with me here. By then my own brief marriage was over and she and I made a happy enough life together until fifteen years ago, she too passed away.

So there I was – a single, ageing orphan of fifty-three, without children or siblings, or any wider family. If I missed such relationships at least my work, as well as being both interesting and challenging, brought me into constant contact with people, young and old. That was the way things stayed until, in my early sixties, I retired.

It was then that I began, like many people at this stage of life, to sort out my house, clearing the accumulations of stuff collected – and neglected – over the years. That was how I came again upon my father's books (mouldering in the attic and long forgotten) and how, thereby, I made the discovery that was to change my life completely.

* * * * *

Tucked into the dust jacket of a biography of Isambard Kingdom Brunel (a book that had obviously not caught my interest as a child) I found a large sealed envelope, browning with age at the edges, which had clearly never been opened. Inside was a document which turned out to be the last will and testament of my grandfather, Henry Grey, who had died not long before his son, in the last year of the war.

How the will came to be where I found it (and who had put it there) remains one of the mysteries of this story – a mystery I am unlikely ever to solve. The will, however, contained the first hint I ever had of an estrangement between my father and my grandfather. As I said earlier, my mother told me very little about my father and she had barely mentioned my grandfather, except to say that she had never met him. I have no idea why, when my father returned from France in 1947, he did not contest the earlier (and only known) will by which his two younger sisters had inherited everything, and in which he was not even mentioned. Perhaps he was too ill. Or perhaps (if he were anything like me) he preferred not to make a fuss and upset everyone. In any case, his father's estate, even if it had *all* come to him, would not have made him a wealthy man.

This 'new' will, however, delivered a bombshell. Most of the wording was the same as in the previous one, but my grandfather had added a codicil where he decreed that a certain house 'built and owned by him' should pass solely to his son.

* * * * *

By the time I made my discovery my aunts, the legatees of the original will, were both dead. It was very puzzling to me that neither my mother nor my aunts had ever spoken of this mysterious house that was now, by the terms of both my parents' wills, mine. Certainly none of them seemed to have been aware of it, which was very strange, as it lay less than twenty miles from the village where I had lived for more than half my lifetime.

Needless to say, I was extremely curious to see it, and once the document was lodged with my solicitor, the legal shenanigans over and the will pronounced valid, I drove out to find it.

That, however, was more easily said than done. In the foothills of the Clwyd Range and just beyond the hamlet of Pentrefechan, the house was completely invisible from the road. Indeed it was so buried in its own garden that, like the prince in *The Sleeping Beauty*, I had to hack my way to it, but when at last I broke through the small forest of silver birch and mountain ash, the brambles and bindweed that had grown and overgrown around it, I stood and gazed in wonder and disbelief.

So this was my inheritance! A house lost in time and place. A house never inhabited and now so derelict it could surely never *be* inhabited. A house (though I could not know it then) containing a secret that was to turn what was left of my life upside down. A house so strange and beautiful that from the very first moment I saw it, I have been bewitched.

II   THE HOUSE

Ty Newydd. New House. That was its name. In reality it was both new (having never been lived in or even finished) and old (having been built nearly a century before).

Knowing full well I would not be able to afford to restore it, I nevertheless called in Glyn Thomas, a builder who had done work for me in the past. From beneath a thatch of unruly grey hair his brown eyes surveyed the house with a despondent look.

"Hopeless," he said. "Riddled with asbestos, see? Used for insulation in those days. The only thing to do with it, Louis, is pull it down." He sighed and chewed at the tatty ends of his moustache. "And given the nature of the problem, that too will cost a fortune."

"No," I said. "This house itself is my fortune! What's more, I love it as it is. I shall leave it to time and nature to finish the job they've already begun and reduce it to a picturesque ruin. Meanwhile it can stand as a memorial to my grandfather."

Glyn Thomas shrugged and stayed silent for a moment before startling me by saying, "To your *Tad* too . . ."

"My father! But he didn't even *know* about it."

"Really?" said Glyn. His dark eyebrows drew together in a questioning frown. "Well now, I don't think that can be right. My old *Taid*, my grandfather, knew old Henry

Grey quite well, both being in the building trade, see? And according to him *your* Taid built this house for his only son. For your father, isn't it?"

Confused by this unexpected and (to me) surprising information, I merely nodded.

"What's more," he went on, "Henry was using the project as a way of teaching his son the skills of his own trade. As soon as the lad left school, they worked on it together. Only long before Henry Llewelyn had completed his apprenticeship he took off!"

"Took off? All this is news to me . . ."

Glyn looked uncomfortable. He glanced at me warily. "Family secrets, is it?" he asked.

"Family history," I amended. "And high time I knew it, I should say. So what more do you know?"

"Well, I don't know much more," Glyn said slowly. An honest and somewhat taciturn man, he was clearly reluctant to embroider or speculate on the story. "All this was long before my time, isn't it? Just things I gleaned from tales *my* Taid told."

"So what did you glean?"

"Your grandfather and father never got on," Glyn resumed. "There were constant fallings-out. Your Taid wanted his son to take on the business and stay here where he belonged, but Henry Llewelyn had no intention of living in this godforsaken corner of nowhere for the rest of his days. He wanted to see the world. Finally there was an almighty row and overnight the boy disappeared. It turned out he had got himself a job with a civil engineering outfit somewhere up north. As far as I know he never came back. Not even when his Tad was dying!"

"Well, he did return briefly," I said, "otherwise I would not be here! And I do know a bit about my father's life from that point on, but of what went before – of his boyhood and youth – I know almost nothing. And I know less than nothing about what happened *here*, to my grandfather and to this house."

"Apparently the old man lost all interest in the house," said Glyn. "He put it on the market, unfinished as it was, and when it failed to sell – it was during the Depression, see, and nothing was selling hereabouts – he simply abandoned it."

* * * * *

Over that first summer I returned again and again to the house. As I wandered through the grounds, sporadically clearing some of the seemingly impenetrable thicket that surrounded it, I wondered about the equally impenetrable puzzles my inheritance had brought with it. I regretted that my mother, never much interested in the past, had left very little documentary evidence of her life. Even my father's wartime letters to her had been destroyed in some annual clear-out, a fact I had always reproached her with, since it robbed me of any glimpse of my father's personality, any distant echo of his voice.

Surely she could not have known about this house? She could never even have known my father *well*. Theirs had been a whirlwind romance. As I said, they had met when he was working on the local aircraft factory and scarcely a year after they were married he was sent first to Scotland and then, after his call-up, all over the country for his basic army training. Immediately that was finished he was posted abroad. During all those years she hardly saw him.

When he returned from France Henry Llewelyn must have been a changed man, sick and crippled, not the handsome, energetic and lively young husband she remembered at all. Perhaps he had never told her about his early life, his alienation from his family and the building of this house. Or perhaps he had told her but, in the trauma of what later happened, she forgot it all.

By the time the summer was waning I had reflected on these matters till I was weary of them. Not so with the house, however. I knew the house both inside and out as well as I knew my own home and the more I saw of it, the more I loved it.

It was a two storey L-shaped building, its red brick already mellowed by age, its Welsh slate roof crusted with patches of golden lichen. The simple, uncluttered design and the high standard of craftsmanship throughout suggested to me that my grandfather had been strongly influenced by the English Arts and Crafts movement.

On the ground floor the casement windows opened into large light and airy rooms, the light made green and gentle by the mantle of foliage masking the verandah. Supported on finely carved wooden pillars, this verandah ran the full length of all the walls except for the one facing north. Over the years it had become laden with entanglements of vine and honeysuckle and an Albertine rose which, in spite of its great age, was still in late summer hung with heavy clusters of coppery pink blooms. Its petals lay like pale confetti on the tiles of the verandah and its blooms scented the air in both house and garden.

Enough. Enough. I could talk about Ty Newydd for ever but would never be able to capture in words the impact its secret, solitary beauty made on me.

* * * * *

During the three months the house had been mine I had succeeded, with the help of Glyn Thomas' wife, Bronwen, in clearing the interior of dirt and debris. Shards of glass from broken windows, dust, mouse droppings and drifts of dead leaves were banished and cobwebs were swept from the ceilings and walls of the rooms. The upper half of these walls, plastered and painted the colour of buttermilk, remained indelibly printed with watery stains and splotches of green mould but the lower half, panelled in natural oak, was undamaged. Bronwen had cleaned, waxed and polished these panels – as well as the oak window seats – to a soft shine. And it was one day in early September, when I was sitting reading in the middle window of the sitting room, that the house sprang its next surprise on me.

A slight stir of the air or a flicker of the light behind me alerted me to some sort of change beyond the verandah and glancing up I saw, leaning against a rowan tree whose berries were already turning scarlet, the figure of a woman.

Completely motionless, she was standing and regarding me with a quiet, steady gaze. If it had been dusk I might have taken her for a ghost because in all the months that I myself had been haunting the house I had never seen another soul there – except, of course, for Bronwen Thomas who had long ago finished her work and no longer came to Ty Newydd.

This woman, in any case, was very different. Older than Bronwen, closer indeed to my own age, she was tall and slender with ash-grey hair drawn back in a short ponytail. At that distance I could not see the colour of her eyes, only that they were dark and wide set, dominating her face. In a grey blouse sprigged with violets, and an ankle-length green skirt, she made me think of a dryad, a spirit of the greenwood that pressed so closely against my walls. It was an impression deepened by the air of stillness and serenity that seemed to emanate from her. I saw that she was conscious of my attention but she did not move.

I swung my legs over the sill and stepped on to the verandah. Fallen rose petals and dry leaves whispered beneath my feet. From the depths of the thicket a single blackbird called. The woman smiled, then, and held out her hand.

"Hello," she said. "I believe you must be Mr. Louis Grey? The owner of Ty Newydd?"

Her eyes were amber brown. Her skirt, as she moved, rustled in the long grass.

"My name is Angharad Hughes," she said. "I do so hope you don't mind me trespassing here. I was told the rightful owner had at last been found, but I could not resist coming here one more time – if only to say farewell. I have loved this place ever since I first saw it as a child."

III   ANGHARAD

It had never occurred to me that at a time of life when I was winding down, living in the past, uncertain of any future, I would find the woman I had been seeking all my life.

My marriage had been brief – and unsatisfactory from the start. With the physical ardour of a young man I had fallen in love with a pretty girl who had been a good tennis player, a conscientious housewife and a chatterbox, but in the long term there had proved to be no viable common ground that my wife and I could share. The passion had soon burnt itself out leaving us with only an increasing burden of mutual irritations.

With Angharad it was very different. In my old-fashioned way I am tempted to say I fell in love with her at first sight. Certainly, even during those few minutes when she introduced herself to me in my garden, I knew I found her both beautiful and intriguing. What's more, from the beginning she seemed to me to belong at Ty Newydd, and within days she had become an essential element in my own love for it. Gently – and, it seemed, inexorably – I was led into an enchanted world I had never before encountered.

We experienced such pleasure, such comfort and completeness when we were together, that it felt as if we had known each other always. Our thoughts and feelings were not necessarily identical but were always compatible. The shared love we had for the house and its garden soon found counterparts in other shared loves – the love of books, of music, of history (especially local history), of gardens in general, of walking the hills – the list grew and grew until it seemed endless.

Time, usually ticking away so fast, slowed down, and as September (a warm, mellow month that year) slid towards October, every day became an adventure. Excited anticipation led to new areas of exploration, the making of fresh discoveries, sometimes mundane, sometimes thrilling and a deepening sense of satisfaction at each day's end.

The base camp for all this exploration was, of course, Ty Newydd. This is where we always met and where, in its total privacy, our relationship grew from fascination through friendship and into love. We were both romantics and dreamers, especially Angharad, so much so that to me it sometimes seemed she came from some other world, an elvish world that exists just out of sight of this one. But she had a very down-to-earth, practical side too. She threw herself enthusiastically into the seemingly unending task of clearing the garden. Working side by side in the bird-haunted peace of Ty Newydd, we spent many hours in animated conversation – and as many others in companionable silence.

Later, as the weather turned colder, we turned our attention to the house. We bought little gifts to it; pieces of pottery, pictures, cushions and small items of furniture purchased in junk and charity shops. Angharad found a delphinium blue teapot and two matching mugs and after I rooted out my old camping stove we could make tea or coffee for ourselves. Then, in an end of season sale, we bought a splendid barbecue that we set up on the verandah, cooking there in all weathers as the twilight thickened and the moon rose, glimmering, through the trees. It was like playing at house. It was a return to childhood. And as we worked and walked and talked together we tracked back through our own histories and heard each other's stories.

* * * * *

Angharad had begun by telling me how she first discovered Ty Newydd when taken there by her grandmother, Megan.

"The day stands out in my memory," she said, "because from the moment I set foot in it I felt somehow connected with this house. My grandmother knew the whole area really well, but even then the house was pretty well buried in greenery and I wondered how she knew it was here. I remember asking her if she had lived in it as a child. She said no – but she didn't explain further. She seemed rather quiet and sad that day. Not at all like her usual self."

"Did she live around here all her life?" I asked.

"Well, never far away," said Angharad. "She was born and spent her childhood in Caer Gawr, but when she left school at fourteen, she went to work as under nursemaid to the Squire's children at Estyn Hall. She was only seventeen when she married my grandfather, John Ferris. He was the head gardener there and was quite a lot older than her. They had a tied cottage on the estate where their two daughters, Sara and Johanna, were born and brought up."

"And which one was your mother?"

"The younger one, Johanna. She trained as a nurse before she married my father in 1953."

"Then you came along!"

"I did. They had me quite quickly but had to wait ten years for my twin brothers to arrive. In the meantime I was an only child . . . and probably spoiled."

Angharad's eyes gleamed at me. This was a characteristic of hers, a sort of hidden, teasing laughter that expressed itself through the changing light in her eyes.

"Just like you," she said.

"I was not spoiled," I protested. "My mother was not the spoiling sort. But I *was* lonely. Weren't you?"

"Not at all. I had my beloved cousin, Liza living close by at Caer Gawr. She was an only child, too, but we practically lived in each other's pockets and made lots of mischief together!"

"I wish I had known you then."

"No, you don't. At that age you would have been properly scornful of two giddy, giggling girls."

"Never!" I said indignantly. "I detest miserable, male misogyny (let's have a competition in alliteration) and I have *never* hated girls. At any age."

Angharad laughed, poured peat-brown tea from our teapot, and blew the steam off her mug.

"Are you still good friends?" I said.

"With Liza? Very much so. She still lives in Caer Gawr. She's been married forever and has four grown-up children."

"And what about *her* mother, your mother's sister Sara?"

"Sara is still alive. And lovely. She was a year older than my mother, but has outlived her by ten years. She's eighty-seven now and very frail. She's in a nursing home in Watstown."

There was a long pause while Angharad sipped her tea and stared into the trees. The clearing we had already done had left a gap between them wide enough for us to see the mountainside. The heather on its flanks, highlighted by the setting sun, glowed like a purple pelt.

"Liza was with me when I first came to this house," she went on dreamily. "We must have been about eight when Nain brought us here."

"Why would your grandmother have done that, d'you think?"

"I don't know. I think perhaps she was minding Liza and me for the day and wanted something to entertain us. She probably thought an abandoned, secret house would appeal to children. She let us poke around the empty rooms for five minutes and then shooed us both into the garden. As I told you, she seemed rather low that day and she stayed indoors, saying she wanted to look for something. That was fine by us. As you can imagine, the garden, with all its potential for hiding places and dens, was a perfect paradise for kids . . ."

"Just as now it's a perfect paradise for us!"

Angharad smiled assent. "It's always been that for me," she said, "though oddly enough Liza seems to have no memory of that day or of this place, and it's one of the few things I don't share with her. Selfishly, I've always wanted to keep it to myself. Clearly it did not affect her the way it did me."

"That sense of belonging, you mean?"

"Perhaps. But it's also odd that *you* should be its inheritor. You, who feel exactly as I do about it, but knew nothing of its existence until a few months ago."

It struck me then, as it had not before, that the inheritance my father left me was growing in size, in significance and in wonder.   For surely if I had not inherited Ty Newydd, I should never have met Angharad. Indeed, in a sense, she was becoming part of my inheritance, and by far the most important and precious part.

* * * * *

In the course of the autumn I learned not only about Angharad's childhood (a happy, family-centred time with no major traumas) but also the basic facts of her adult life. Like most of our generation she had gone travelling the world in her early twenties, backpacking through India and later throughout Europe.   When she returned, her brothers were heading for university and she decided to take that path too.

She read history at Aberystwyth and then trained as a librarian, working in various libraries until she met her husband, David Hughes. They married in 1980, moved to England, had a son, Elwyn, in 1982 and a daughter, Sophie, in 1986.

This very bare outline of Angharad's life was filled out by her with amused and amusing accounts of the sort of family accidents and incidents familiar to us all. Through them I was able to glean some impression of the personalities involved.

Her husband, like me, had been a teacher, a steady, faithful and reliable man. To me, reading between the lines, it seemed that he might perhaps have been a bit pedestrian, not given to flights of fancy or sudden impetuosities. Indeed, I sensed in Angharad a lingering disappointment, an awareness of something missing in their marriage. She had loved her husband, but I never doubted that her love for me was of a different order, fulfilling longings in her that had been unacknowledged or even repressed. She was too loyal to David's memory ever to confess this but I detected from a hundred small signs (to which, as a lover, I was sensitive) that the closeness *we* shared was for her, as it was for me, an exquisitely new and exciting experience.

Tragically, twenty years previously, David had died in a car accident. It was then that Angharad's cousin Liza had persuaded her to return to this area, where she would have the support of her family.

In time Angharad became head librarian in Watstown library and, but for the recent closures and cutbacks, she would still have been there. Disgusted as I am by governmental cheeseparing, for me personally that particular example of it was a blessing. After all, it was Angharad's early retirement that allowed her to spend so much time at Ty Newydd – and with me.

* * * * *

It was late December. Ice crunched in the long tussocky grass of the orchard as Angharad and I shuffled a heavy wooden ladder into place beneath an apple tree. The light was cold and very clear. There was no sun, just a luminous veil of fine, high cloud beyond which we could see the faintest suggestion of blue. The orchard lay on the far side of the garden and through the contorted boughs of its ancient trees the mountainside looked very close; a patchwork of rusty bracken, grey rock and winter-bleached turf.

"This is where I'd like us to build our house," she said, testing the stability of the ladder against a branch. "Just here." Against the dark wood her crimson sweater stood out like a dark flame, warming the air around her.

We had come a long way since September. Plans for a spring wedding were already advanced. Angharad's son Elwyn and daughter Sophie were still reeling from the shock but were teasingly supportive. They addressed me as PSD – 'Prospective Step-Dad' – and, childless as I was, I felt a thrill at the title while being very aware that we were still only in the shallows of our relationship. By now, however, my feelings for Angharad were as deep as the tarn at the summit of the mountain. And that was said to be bottomless.

"Are you going to climb this thing – or me?" Angharad asked, breaking into my thoughts and indicating the ladder against the tree.

I set my foot on the first rung. It seemed solid. We were after the mistletoe that grew in such profusion among the top branches that it was more a mistletoe tree than an apple tree.

"Sure, we'll build here," I agreed, going up, "but this tree has to stay. We'd offend the pagan gods if we cut it down."

"We'll get a new ladder, though," she said.

* * * * *

Back at the house we put the mistletoe into a chipped Victorian ewer we had come across when searching the outhouses for the ladder. Ty Newydd now was furnished after a fashion with the bits and pieces we had brought to it and it looked like a vestigial home.

"Strange," Angharad observed. "Inexplicable really, the way I've always felt here. My conviction that I have some deep connection with this house.

"Me, too," I said. "As you know."

"Well, *you* do, of course," she said. "After all, your Taid and your Tad built it together."

We had both accepted that we could not live at Ty Newydd, but our plan was to sell both our own houses and with the proceeds engage Glyn Thomas to build us a new one in the grounds. Thus my grandfather's house would remain part of our domain. Meanwhile, although our shared world had expanded, we still came here as often as we could. It would make a good base for supervising the construction of the house we had just decided to call *Perllan* (The Orchard). Ty Newydd itself, however, remained our secret hideout. We had told no-one of its existence, not even her children.

"This Christmas time," she had suggested, "we'll hold a pre-Christmas party here. A celebration. We'll invite the kids, Liza and her brood and anyone *you* would like to join us . . ."

I shook my head. "There's no-one," I said. "Except maybe Glyn and Bronwen Thomas. Otherwise I think it should be a strictly family affair . . ."

I had never been a great party person but I was looking forward to this one and especially to meeting Liza and *her* family for the first time.

Angharad set the ewer of heavily-berried mistletoe on the window seat and went into the kitchen. There was no water or electricity out there, nothing at all except for an oak dresser (made with the same care as the wooden fittings in the rest of the house) and a small table on which the camping stove and our supplies all stood. I could hear her making hot chocolate for us and while she was busy I lit the fire we had laid in the sitting room grate. The kindling flared into life and the dry old apple tree logs I had sawn up as we began to clear the orchard soon caught. The chimney worked well, was not blocked with birds' nests or other rubbish as I had feared, and the flames leapt up. The dusk retreated and light flickered over the walls, setting the shadows dancing. The room filled with the elusive scent of burning applewood.

I sat down on our only chair (a simple Van Gogh-type thing with a frayed rope bottom) and Angharad returned with our blue mugs. She handed me one and moved towards the hearth. The fireplace was built of brick with a short low projection like a seat on either side. These were both topped with a deep oaken board similar to the window seats. She turned to brush the dust off one before sitting down, but as she lowered herself on to it, the board wobbled and a fine trickle of dust leaked out on to the floor.

"Oops!" she said, leaping up. "Not sure this is safe. The cement seal must have crumbled."

She tested it again by pushing at the wood and, sure enough, the whole top slid sideways. Carefully she lifted it off, set it against the wall and peered into the space beneath.

"It's hollow," she said, "but there's some sort of package stuffed inside."

I stood up to join her as she reached down and brought out a rough parcel wrapped in a piece of old-fashioned oilcloth. There was no thunderclap, no tremble in the air, no split second of premonition, but when Angharad peeled back the cloth she revealed something that was to change my life – both our lives – radically once more.

With a little gasp she lifted out a bundle of letters, the envelopes dusty and yellowed with age and the whole lot tied together with a faded red ribbon. We looked at them and we looked at each other, curious and intrigued. But neither of us suspected then (how could we?) that this discovery was to herald yet another instalment of my inheritance.

IV   *THE LETTERS*

We let the fire burn down to ash, tidied up and left Ty Newydd. Both of us were troubled and uneasy. Clearly the letters we had found hidden away and tied in a red silk ribbon had been both precious and private. One glance at their contents had indeed confirmed them as love-letters, and by the addresses on the envelopes we already suspected a connection with ourselves. Did we have the right to read them? Or should we place them on the embers of the fire and watch as they burned away, taking whatever revelations and secrets they contained with them?

"I need time to think," said Angharad, "and, anyway, the light in here, with only the firelight and a couple of candles, will not be good enough to read them properly."

"My house or yours, then?"

Mine was further away, but Angharad said that if we went to Llaneudaf we could pick up a take-away in Bryn Afon. When we arrived, my small stone-built cottage in the lee of the churchyard wall seemed stale, cold and comfortless. I was rarely there these days.

However, the meal and a bottle of red wine warmed us as well as giving us time to think and talk. It was nine o'clock when we cleared the table, spread the envelopes across it in chronological order and sat down.

The postmarks, where legible, were mostly for 1928, spanning the months from August to December. Only the final two were marked 1929. The letters themselves, written on lined paper torn from an exercise book – his – or on plain blue notepaper – hers – were undated, except occasionally the day of the week was jotted down. Hers were longer, written in a neat schoolgirl script – and in Welsh. His were short, concentrated, spattered with blobs of ink where the nib of the pen had been pressed down too hard in his haste, and written in a mixture of bad Welsh and good English. Hers were signed *Meg*, with a long tail of kisses. His ended simply with *Yours for ever and ever and ever, Hal.* Sometimes he had added a skilful little cartoon drawing of a place or a person.

"Meg," sighed Angharad. She removed her spectacles and rubbed her eyes. "Megan Jones. My grandmother. It has to be! They're addressed to Estyn Hall, where she worked. And although Jones is a common name around here . . ."

Her voice trailed off and then grew firm again as she said, "I reckon this package is what Nain was looking for when she brought Liza and me here all those years ago".

"Right," I said. I felt hollow, my thoughts and feelings in turmoil from the opposing stresses of surprise, bewilderment, excitement and dread that had assailed me from the moment we had found the letters. I looked again at the address on the other envelopes.

"That was my grandfather's house," I said, handing one of them to Angharad. "But the letter's addressed to Henry *Llewelyn* Grey . . . my *father*."

We stared at each other. Angharad was pale and I could feel the colour draining out of my own face.

"So these love-letters were between . . ."

"*My* grandmother," she said, taking a long swig of wine, "and *your* father."

Maybe it was the wine or else the incongruity of the idea of 'father' and 'grandmother' as lovers, but Angharad giggled. I glanced again at the final letter.

"1929," I said. "He was nineteen."

"And my Nain even younger. Sixteen perhaps? Seventeen? *Duw Maur*! God Almighty!"

It was the first time I had ever heard Angharad swear, and this time it was I who laughed. Angharad spoke Welsh, but I did not: hence it was to her that the task of reading the letters had to be left.

* * * * *

Early the next day we returned to Ty Newydd. The weather had changed. A mischievous wind blew sudden squalls of rain at the windows and hooted in the chimney. I relit the fire, moved the kitchen table into the sitting room, settled Angharad there with the letters, then busied myself decorating the room in readiness for our party on Christmas Eve. We had brought a twisted apple bough indoors, fixed it in a large pot and put together a collection of green and gold baubles. I hung these from the twigs and wreathed the whole thing in ropes of ivy to which I attached small bunches of holly and the mistletoe, its berries glowing softly like clouded pearls.

It was a strange day. We sustained ourselves on strong coffee, chunks of cheese, hunks of bread, and apples. By the end of it we had gained powerful impressions of the long-ago young lovers, two strong and engaging personalities. Megan's character was expressed through lively snippets of life at Estyn Hall, through her lightness of tone and through the underlying seriousness of her assessments of people and her hopes for the future.

"I recognize my Nain in these letters," said Angharad. "She could talk for England – though usually in Welsh – and was a great teller of tales. She loved gossip, but hated the malicious kind. She would have been appalled by its prevalence today through the Internet! Even in old age (when most of us get cynical) Nain believed in the essential goodness of people – and indeed of life itself . . ."

Henry Llewelyn was perhaps less mature. ("Typical boy," said Angharad). He was full of enthusiasm for a range of interests: fishing, reading and his plans to become an engineer and build bridges like Telford and Brunel. He was scornful of his 'stick-in-the-mud' father, but expressed that mostly through witty observations –and more rarely in fiery outbursts of irritation. Towards Megan he showed an endearing and enduring tenderness. *My cariad of cariads*, he called her. His letters moved me deeply. After all, it was my first direct encounter with my father.

"I think I'd have liked him," I said, after Angharad had read me one passage, a boyish flight of fancy in which he had imagined their future together. "But it's odd thinking of him as Hal. My mother never referred to him by that name. And what's even stranger for me as an elderly man, is first meeting my father as a *young* man. It does weird things to my perceptions. Puts an entirely new inter-pretation on the saying 'the child is father to the man.'"

It was the final two letters, however, that shook us to our roots. I already knew from what Glyn Thomas had told me that 1929 was the year in which my father and grandfather had a quarrel so grave that my father left home for good. But whereas Glyn had thought it was to do with the house and Henry Llewelyn's rejection of his father's plans, these last letters revealed an altogether different story.

Outside the wind had dropped and the light was fading. Angharad was tired and although we had brought a gas camping lamp with us her eyes were feeling the strain of reading the faint and faraway marks on the paper. Her Welsh was unpractised and probably her brain was weary too. I was back on the window seat, watching the shadows sweep like a slow tide into the spaces between the trees. High up on the mountainside a light twinkled and I was just wondering whether it came from a farm or a cottage when I heard her spring up with an exclamation.

"*Beichiog*! " she cried. "No! Never! Surely?"

"What? What is it? "

I, too, jumped up.

"*Beichiog*," she said again. "It means pregnant. In her last letter Meg is telling your father she is pregnant!"

* * * * *

Megan's final letter was distressed. It was her longest letter and the bright tone had altogether gone. In those days, for an unmarried girl, getting pregnant was a disaster. At the very least she faced dismissal from her job at Estyn Hall. At worst, her family would discard her, tell her never to darken their doors again. Only at the end did she revive a little. She expressed trust and hope in Henry Llewelyn's love for her, his sense of honour and his ability to rescue them both.

We approached *his* last letter with trepidation but found her trust was not initially misplaced. My father said straight away that he would marry her. Wasn't that what they wanted anyway? If people objected, they would elope. They would leave this benighted corner of Wales.

He would get a job. In answer to an earlier enquiry he already had a promising letter from a Scottish firm of civil engineers, and as soon as that was all sorted out they would marry, rent a cottage somewhere . . . he would look after her.

In the final sentence he wrote, "I will speak to my father tonight, *cariad*. Don't worry. All will be well."

That seemed to be it. But as Angharad tucked the letter back into its envelope she found another torn scrap of paper in there. Henry Llewelyn had written a postscript, much blotted and with deep scorings where he had underlined words and phrases. From this it was clear that his confidence in his father had been misplaced. All had been very far from well.

"My father," he wrote, *"is a <u>bastard!</u> He's totally unreasonable. <u>Evil!</u> He was beside himself with fury and said my mother would have been ashamed of me, would be turning in her grave. He called your family a bunch of nobodies and <u>both</u> of us names <u>I would never repeat</u>. He said there was <u>no question</u> of us marrying and that until I was twenty-one his word was law. He shouted that I had not even completed my apprenticeship, and how did I think I could support a wife, let alone a wife and child? The row was terrible, cariad, and went on all night. But I would not give in and when he left for work this morning, he told me to pack up my "paltry goods and chattels" (his words) and clear out. He said he never*

wanted to set eyes on me again. As if I cared! I never want to see him again either!

At this point, Henry Llewelyn ran out of space. He concluded briefly by saying he was leaving that day but would come back for Megan.

"Just as soon as I can get a job, my darling, I will return."

V   SARA

After two almost sleepless nights going over and over the letters, Angharad and I agreed that there were two outstanding questions to which we desperately needed the answers. Firstly, why did my father, Henry Llewelyn, not return to rescue Megan as he had promised? And secondly, was the child they conceived ever born and, if so, what happened to it? We seemed to have reached a dead end.

On the 22nd December, we were back at Ty Newydd. It was looking very festive. The 'tree' stood in an alcove beside the fireplace, apple logs were stacked on the hearth and mistletoe hung from the ceiling light fittings. Somehow we had found time to clean the house and to buy supplies of drink and nibbles for our party.

"There's only one thing I can think of," said Angharad, as we checked the details.

"What? What have we missed?"

"Nothing. It's not that. I meant in relation to our problem."

"Ah!" I put my arm around her. "We must try to forget it," I urged. "The whole story is studded with unanswered questions and unresolved puzzles. I guess we have to accept that."

"But this is a big one. I want so much to know. Has it not struck you, Louis, that if that child was born, he or she would be your half-sibling?"

"Of course. I had realised *that*. But he or she would be ancient, *cariad*. Twenty years older than me. Decrepit at best. Dead most likely."

Light-headed with weariness, we laughed, but then she said, "There is one person who might know something. One last chance perhaps. My aunt Sara. Liza's mother."

I suppose the thing most important to me by then was to restore my faith in my father's honesty and integrity. To clear his name of any slur, any suggestion that he had been a cad. I remained stubbornly certain that he would not have deserted Megan, that he had been an honest and honourable young man and that the passionate feeling he displayed in his letters to her had been genuine and sincere. Indeed, I was more concerned about that than I was about a possible lost sibling. What's more, I was very doubtful that Angharad's aunt would be able to help. If she knew anything about this early love of her mother's why had she not said something years ago? Also, shamefully, I have to confess I was appalled at the thought of visiting her in her nursing home. Such places depressed me utterly. They were approaching too close for comfort on my own horizon. To please Angharad, however, I agreed to accompany her.

* * * * *

We drove to Watstown through lightly falling snow. The roof of the Victorian vicarage that had recently been converted to a nursing home was powdered with it, but otherwise it was dissolving as fast as it fell. Indoors the atmosphere was jolly, garish decorations everywhere, a huge, overburdened tree in the elegant hallway. We were welcomed by a pretty girl whose English was good but heavily accented with an eastern European flavour.

Sara's room was square, light and pleasant, made homely by pictures and ornaments that had obviously come from her own home. Christmas cards covered the window ledge but there were no other decorations. Through the window there was a distant view of our mountain.

Sara sat in a high-backed chair. Her feet, neatly clad in laced black shoes, rested on an embroidered footstool. She was tiny, shrunk perhaps with age, but upright and alert. Her silver hair was short cropped and curly, her face as brown and craggy as a walnut shell. She recognised Angharad at once and gave her a warm smile. Me, she studied gravely for an embarrassingly long minute.

"I hear you are engaged to be married," she said.

Her voice was husky, lightly scored with Welsh rhythms and cadences. She spoke very distinctly and was clearly (to my relief) fully in possession of her mental faculties.

The Polish girl (she came from Gdansk, she told us) brought us tea and small butterfly cakes. I sat on the only other chair in the room, Angharad on the bed. Snow continued to drift past the window and was starting to settle on the rhododendrons in the garden and the winter light gradually dimmed as we talked. It took time and tact. Angharad had decided to tell her aunt that she was writing a family history. This was true in intention but not yet begun in fact. It was a strategy that gave her the excuse for questioning Sara about the past in general and about her mother in particular. Slowly, painfully, we discovered that Sara did have the answers to all our questions. Or almost. Because in the end there was one crucial question that *we* were able to answer for *her*.

* * * * *

At first Sara talked quite happily about her childhood. She confirmed that she was born in 1930, the eldest daughter of Megan and John Ferris; that her sister, Johanna (Angharad's mother) was born only fifteen months later; that they had enjoyed a settled and happy childhood in the cottage allotted to them by John's employer, the Squire of Estyn Hall; that although John was considerably older than Megan he had been an involved, playful and affectionate father.

"It was idyllic, I suppose," she said. "All that parkland and the gardens to play in – gardens that my Tad attended with great skill and devotion. He was a lovely man: dependable, patient, rather quiet, but with a mischievous sense of humour. He let Mam do all the talking. He thought the sun shone out of Mam!"

It was then, when Angharad took this up and nudged her aunt towards talking about Megan, that we both sensed some reserve, some uneasiness even, in Sara.

"Well, "she said. "She was a good mother, very conscientious. She had a fund of funny stories and was an excellent cook. She was lively and loving . . . and . . ."

She hesitated, and daringly Angharad voiced the un- spoken 'but' we both felt was there. Sara frowned.

"But nothing really," she said. "Nothing important anyway. It was just something Jo and I sensed as we grew older . . . some mild – but chronic and incurable – sadness in her . . . something we could not understand or reach."

"Oh," Angharad was clearly unsure how to go on. I fidgeted, suspecting that we were trespassing on forbidden ground but unable, of course, to intervene.

Sara glanced at me and then shifted her gaze to Angharad, where it lingered. "I'm guessing," she said softly, "that you want the whole story, the full truth, any skeletons imprisoned in the family cupboard let out?"

Angharad nodded and Sara picked up her lukewarm tea. "It was not until my mother lay dying," she resumed at last, "that she told me . . . and *only* me, mind . . ."

"Told you . . . ?" Angharad prompted as Sara paused to drink her tea.

"Told me," Sara's voice quavered, "the truth about myself. That I was not . . . not actually . . . my father's daughter."

The silence in Sara's room was palpable. I could *feel* Angharad's breath stalled in her chest. Below us in the hall we heard the grandfather clock strike four. Then, in a rush, the rest of the story came.

Sara's biological father, she told us, had disappeared six months before she was born. When her family discovered Megan's 'shameful' pregnancy they had insisted, in spite of her protestations that her lover intended to return, that she accept John Ferris' generous offer of marriage. He, apparently, had been in love with her ever since the day she entered the Squire's service and was happy to take on the responsibility for another man's child as long as he could have *her*. The wedding took place in July 1929 and later, within days of her birth in January 1930, he had officially adopted Sara.

To hide my shock (for I had not foreseen this) I stood up and wandered to the window. I watched the snowflakes whirling in the twilight, felt that their wild tumult gave visible expression to the turmoil in my head and heart. It struck me then, that my inheritance was like a snowball rolling down a hill, gathering size and substance as it went. I found it hard to take in this latest accretion. The fact that this frail old lady, never encountered before today and now sitting silent in her chair, was my own father's daughter, was my *sister* . . .

"So who . . . ?" whispered Angharad. "Who *was* your father?"

From our point of view this was an unnecessary question. We both already knew.

"I don't know," Sara said. "I've *never* known."

The words were emphatic, and her voice was strong but blurred, perhaps by unshed tears. "I did not *want* to know. I wished my mother had taken her secret to the grave. I *loved* my Tad, my *known* father. Loved him passionately. I wanted him and him only to *be* my father. I had spent my life modelling myself on him, revelling in the ways in which I saw myself as like him. And I wanted Johanna to be my *full* sister. I hated this unknown man who had robbed me of the woman I believed I was – this man who was nothing to me! I was sixty years old with a grown-up daughter of my own and four grandchildren when I discovered that my whole life had been a deceit, a lie . . ."

"No!" cried Angharad, upset herself now and, like me, bitterly regretting that we had desired the release of this particular skeleton from its cupboard. She leapt up and went to comfort her aunt. They murmured softly together while I, the unacknowledged cause of the distress, stayed stupidly staring into the turbulent dark.

How much later it was I do not know. Time had collapsed in on itself. Angharad had eventually switched on the lamps and gone downstairs to fetch another cup of tea for her aunt. Sara had fallen into a doze. I crossed the room and squatted by her chair, studied her face, took her gnarled old hand in mine. She woke with a start, sat up immediately and looked down at me with a gaze as direct and open as Angharad's.

"It's been lovely to meet you, Louis," she said. "I'm sorry about the family history: so boring for an outsider."

I swallowed, and stayed dumb. A small wry smile tweaked at the corners of her mouth. Still I said nothing. I felt totally inadequate to the situation. Behind me I heard the door open and Angharad came in. She joined us, set the tea on the table, handed Sara a small glass of whisky and sank to the floor beside us.

"Would it help, Aunt Sara," she said, "if we told you your natural father was a good man – that he fully intended to return and marry Megan – that he only failed because by the time he was in a position to do so, she was already married to John?"

Sara took a sip of whisky. "Possibly," she said. "In some ways. But Johanna – your Mam – knew nothing about this. So how would *you* know, *cariad*?"

"I . . . that is, Louis and I . . . found their letters to each other . . . at Ty Newydd."

Sara turned from one to the other of us.

"I knew there was more to this," she said, "more than you've admitted. I suspected all along that your Louis did not simply come here today to be introduced as your future husband." With some asperity in her voice she went on, "I've told you the truth, all the truth I know. Perhaps now *you* should do the same?"

"Only if you think you can bear it," said Angharad. Direct gaze met direct gaze. Sara downed the rest of the whisky.

"Fortified with that," she said, "I believe I can bear it."

Angharad reached across her and took my hand.

"You rightly guessed," she said, "that Louis had an ulterior motive in coming with me. He has a direct interest in your story, you see, because it is linked with his own. But what you have told us is as much a shock to him as it is to me. He is the man I love, Aunt Sara, and he too is a good man. The fact is that Louis . . . Louis is the son of *your* natural father. Born twenty years later and to a different mother. Louis, my darling, is your brother, your half-brother . . ."

My heart was jumping so hard I was convinced they could hear it. I was afraid Angharad had moved too quickly, gone too far, too fast. Sara switched her look from her niece to me. Her blue eyes, faded to grey, filled with tears, but she seized my other hand, squeezed it hard and smiled.

VI   FINALE

The party was in full swing. Indoors, Ty Newydd rang
with the music and laughter that had been denied it for
nearly ninety years. Outside, an inch of snow turned the
garden into a Christmas card wonderland. Angharad
looked bewitching in a long, softly-flowing, leaf-green
dress, recalling my first impression of her as a dryad. I met
Liza and her four entertaining children, discovering in a
couple of hours that these new relations of mine had,
between them, a myriad of skills and talents. Mostly, it
seemed on that day, for making a great deal of noise!

Sara did not come. She and Liza thought it might be too
much for her. There would, with luck, be time for us to get
to know each other later; for her to read the letters for
herself and make our father's acquaintance as I had; for her
to see that he was not the villain she had imagined for so
many years – and maybe to forgive him. I planned to bring
her here to Ty Newydd in the spring when the garden
woke again. I hoped that in this peaceful place, so much
part of our history, we might be able to reclaim for
ourselves something of the long, lost years that lay between us.

After toasts had been drunk, carols sung and Christmas
wishes shared and exchanged, Angharad's children,
Elwyn and Sophie, hauled me away from a conversation
with Liza's eldest son and stood me in front of the tree.

178

"Come on, PSD," said Sophie. "Tell us the story of how your tiny inheritance grew and flourished 'like a green bay tree.'"

"A family tree," I amended. "Surely you don't want to hear it again. How many times will that be?"

"At least a score," said Elwyn, refreshing my glass.

"Old people get so tedious," I protested, "endlessly telling the same stories, meandering through the past . . ."

"This isn't the past," said Sophie. "It's the present. And if you're going to marry Mum you must prove your credentials."

"My . . . what?" I asked.

I was slightly pickled, made stupid and diffuse by a heady mixture of champagne and joy.

"Your credentials," they chorused.

"Well," I began. "It all started with a tatty old collection of books, more specifically with a biography of Isambard Kingdom Brunel –" (cheers) "– in which I found my grandfather's latest will. And through that will I discovered I owned this wonderful house." (More cheers). And in this house I met your even more wonderful mother, Angharad –" (cheers and jeers) "– and together, in this house, we came upon your great-grandmother Megan's letters to my father, Henry Llewellyn Grey. And his to her!"

By now the racket was tremendous and the disturbance brought down a sprig of mistletoe from the ceiling. There was laughter and more cheers. Someone plucked at a guitar and started to sing *My love is like a red, red rose*, while someone else pushed Angharad to join me. She picked up the fallen mistletoe, waved it over my head, kissed me hard and flapped her hands to quieten everyone so that I could finish.

"– and through those letters," I continued, "we uncovered our secret, shared history which opened up for me (a confirmed, solitary, childless and miserable old bachelor) this large, rumbustious, raucous and undisciplined family, the individuals of which I have still the pleasurable – ha! – prospect of getting to know . . ."

"Just as well it was our mother you fell for," Sophie shouted from the back of the room. "If it had been *Liza*, you'd have been wanting to marry your half-niece. Is that even allowable?"

"Especially since *she's* married already," said Elwyn.

More cheers and whistles and cat-calls before quietness was restored.

"Thank you," I said. I had sobered up a bit by then. "Maybe most importantly of all," I added, "after sixty-eight years of being an orphan I made contact (through his letters) with the father I never knew and met a sister I did not even know existed. My originally worthless inheritance has grown and grown, bringing me riches of a kind beyond price – and way beyond my wildest dreams."

* * * * *

We stood on the verandah, leaning into each other for warmth and the sheer pleasure of physical contact even through our thick winter jackets.

Behind us Ty Newydd was quiet again, the candles extinguished, the fire doused, the clutter removed, the rooms restored to their near-century of peace.

"That was so lovely," murmured Angharad.

"Wasn't it?"

I kissed the top of her head, getting a mouthful of woollen fibres from the pom-pom on her hat. The sky was strewn with stars like a daisy field and the moon, lurking behind the trees, created a romantic pattern of shifting light and shadow over house and garden.

"You're right about your inheritance," she mused. "Beginning like a tree with a tiny seed, then growing and branching out in unexpected and astonishing ways."

"Lots of serendipity," I agreed. "In fact, serendipity in spades!"

Angharad turned her face up to the moon. "Gifts of the capricious gods," she said, "perhaps not to be altogether trusted?"

We were both silent. I daresay she, like me, was reflecting that time was not on our side and that Chance, which had brought us together, could just as easily separate us. With that sad and unwelcome thought it struck me, too, how short a time it was since we had met and for how brief a period we had known one another. I trembled to think how little she knew of my manifold imperfections.

"I feel I must warn you," I said impulsively. "I'm not always as level-headed and equable as you have so far experienced me. I can be grumpy and quick tempered. Sometimes pernickety, too, from having spent so long on my own . . ."

"Well, as for that," she countered, "if we are in confessional mode – I know I can seem moody occasionally. Just as long as you remember it will be no fault of yours, Louis. It's simply a need I have at times to withdraw from company, an overwhelming desire for quietness, for introspection." She paused and then added with a quiver of laughter in her voice, "Also, I keep all the clocks in the house five minutes fast – which used to irritate my husband no end . . ."

We laughed and drew apart a little. "All will be well," I said firmly. "All manner of things will be well. We will live the love of our lives in a way denied to Henry Llewelyn Grey and Megan Jones. What they lost we have found . . . Ty Newydd . . . each other . . . and a whole family that would never have existed but for them . . ."

Angharad stepped off the verandah, took my hand in hers and drew me after her. Slowly we walked through the trees. The path was lit by the eerie luminosity that snow gives off, and by the moon playing peek-a-boo through the branches – and as we approached the end of the garden I thought I saw two figures break from the shadows and flit ahead of us.

"Look," I whispered.

"Oh!" breathed Angharad.

But before we could be sure that they were there, they met and merged and melted away into the darkness. At the same moment, ringing clearly through the cold, crisp air, the church clock in the valley began the strokes of midnight. I slid my arm round Angharad and she turned into my embrace.

"Happy Christmas," we said.

LETTER TO A YOUNGER SELF

Dear Ella,

It is many decades since I saw you in my mirror, but this morning, as the soft dawn light crept through my windows, I caught sudden sight of you there again. As is usual nowadays, I had slept badly and was scarcely conscious, but the vision, strange and unexpected as it was, startled me awake.

Instead of my skin, wrinkled like antique crêpe and blotched with brown splodges, I saw your sixteen-year-old face, smooth as cream and flushed with rose. Instead of peering into eyes faded to the colour of watered-down milk, I was riveted by your intense blue-eyed gaze. And instead of hair straggling in thin grey strands across my shoulders, I watched, astonished, as the first beams of the sun turned your heavy tresses to pure gold . . .

This glimpse of you, momentary (and false!) as it was, has haunted me all day, and trailing in its wake have come memories which, like all such re-entries into the past, have overwhelmed me with potent and contradictory sensations of joy and pain.

Here, at the day's end, jaded by age and weary with the continuing demands of my life, I nevertheless feel impelled to pin these recollections down, to examine the thoughts they provoke and to share them with you. Hence this letter.

How beautiful you seem to me now as I contemplate you wandering through the fields and woods of our father's demesne, dreaming, singing, dancing – to a music only you can hear. How beautiful, but how simple!

Those dreams that set you singing are the dreams (so alluring, so enduring!) that dwell in the heart of every girl. Moreover, as you are soon to discover, they are so perfectly encapsulated in the story that bears your name, that (regurgitated and re-imagined in a million copy-cat versions) they continue to captivate all generations . . .

Yet how at odds such dreams are with the realities of life! Just think how far they are from the facts of your own: the hard labour imposed on you by a cruel stepmother and her ugly, bullying daughters; the daily grind of sweeping and scrubbing their kitchen floor, of paring the muddied vegetables and preparing the bloodied meat for their table; the endless trips to the well for water to launder their finery – and to the outhouse for the fuel that creates the ashes amongst which they force you to sleep.

I can only suppose (for I cannot actually remember) that the dreams are an escape from the poverty, the punishments and the mockery you constantly suffer; from the grief of losing a mother; and from the yearning for a father who unaccountably disappeared from your story without trace (and who can blame him?) before it even began.

More stoical, generous and forgiving than I am, you sew until your fingers bleed the exotic dresses your sisters demand for the parties and balls they attend. You encourage them to believe themselves beautiful while at the same time you accept the rags they give *you* to wear and the masking of your own beauty under the layers of grime that cling to you from your bed among the cinders.

What a saint you are, Ella! But what a simpleton!

And yet . . . and yet . . . how I envy you!

As I sit here beside the king (once handsome, once *charming* – now bald and bad-tempered) the weight of my hollow crown bears down on my aching head, and I envy you your dreams, still unfulfilled. They are a means of survival and even a source of joy. Whereas, fulfilled – as they now are in me – they are merely a source of disappointment, regret and bitter memories.

A moment ago I set down my pen and glanced out of the castle window. Stretching into the distance I could see the kingdom I gained by marrying my prince. And believe me it is very much a *king*dom. It has *never*, even remotely, been a *queen*dom. Thinking of this, I sighed. At once the king turned and scowled at me, demanding to know when I would finish my bloody scribbling and what the hell I was doing anyway . . .

Ah, yes, I envy you!

I envy you those summer mornings in the garden with the sun just rising over the mountains and the sweet scent of the flowers released by the overnight rain. I envy you the first exquisite song of the blackbird from the apple tree where the fruit is beginning to blush with ripeness. I envy you those shy conversations with the gardener's boy who sometimes brings you strawberries (still warm from the sun) wrapped in a cabbage leaf. I envy you the quiet winter evenings by the kitchen embers, when the dogs creep in and snuggle among your skirts. I envy you the shared laughter with the cook who tells you fantastical stories before dropping to sleep with her head on the table – leaving you to dream . . .

If I were able, dear younger self (from the unimaginable distance that now lies between us) to advise you, it would be to dream a different dream.

Avoid the commonplace desire for fame and fortune and the seductive influence of a romantic tale, and invest your dreams in your self, in your own unique powers and potential. Consider and care for the wonderful world you love, the world that in my time is threatened as never before. Discover and develop your particular talents (for however small they seem to you now, if you nourish them they will grow) and pay more attention to the gardener's boy who is (above all) considerate, kind and loving, who will never seek power over others and who believes absolutely in the equality of the sexes!

Finally, observe other people well, ask uncomfortable questions and keep an open mind about everything.

And in those quiet times by the swept hearth, when you can briefly relax from care, listen and learn from the cook, who knows how to tell a good and *original* story.

STAIRWAY TO HEAVEN

They had always intrigued her, those steps. She first encountered them when, as a six-year-old, she had been evacuated to the city during the war.

"Mind they blessed steps," warned Mrs. Braithwaite, the kindly woman who had briefly given her a home. "They be right rackety. Dangerous! Don't 'ee try to run down 'em, my lover, or you'll come a cropper!"

Looking at them now, nearly seventy years later, Olga assessed their cracked stones and the towering, patched grey walls that shadowed them. At the top there was a contrasting brightness where light fell on a white wall as the stairway turned.

"I'd hesitate to climb them now," she muttered.

It had not been the dangerous state of the steps that had deterred her as a child, but rather a fear of the witch who lived in the unseen lair beyond them. It was on her way to school one dull November morning that she had first glimpsed this witch. The shadow of a tall conical hat against that white wall, the head of a broomstick being shaken over the top step, the faint cackle of laughter echoing down the stairwell . . . these things put together had sent her fleeing along the street.

Looking up the steps now and noting the odd position of the handrail (or was it merely of a length of old piping? – her eyes were not so good nowadays), Olga took in the two sealed doorways alcoved into the wall, the rusty lamp hanging above the archway, the drape of black cloths, hanging like bats' wings from an invisible hook. Even today, on a bright May day, the steps spooked her slightly.

As she stood, lost in thought, the words of Mr. Braithwaite suddenly returned to her. He had been a funny, grandfatherly man and when she had confided in him about the witch, he had laughed and given her a hug.

"There's nought to be afeared of up there," he had said, "and there be no such thing as witches. That's fairy-tale nonsense. You read too many stories, maidy! Those steps go nowhere." He had paused and ruffled her hair. "I do mind, though, that when I were a nipper we used to call them 'the Stairway to Heaven'".

His words had not convinced her, but eventually something . . . something . . . had made her summon up the courage to explore the stairway.

Olga frowned now and closed her eyes, concentrating, but she could not recall what the trigger had been, only that she had been desperate to conquer her cowardice as well as curious about where the steps ended. On her way to school one day she had stopped at their foot, taken a deep breath and begun the ascent.

Her legs, she remembered, had felt boneless and her heart had hammered so hard against her ribs it had hurt, when, just before the turning, she had heard the slow creaking of a door being stealthily opened. She had stopped and listened, her breath coming in panicky gasps. The creaking, too, stopped, but was followed at once by a hoarse growling mutter that grew louder . . . and drew nearer . . .

She had turned, then, and run, leaping over broken treads and lurching from wall to wall. Her schoolbag, shaken by her erratic movement, had flown open, scattering books and papers everywhere. Sobbing with terror, she had snatched them up and tumbled out into the street.

"Devil on your heels, is he?" someone had laughed as she cannoned into him.

That had been the last time she had seen the Stairway to Heaven. The next day, her mother had arrived at the Braithwaite's house and taken her back home to London. Her father, fighting far away in an African desert, had been killed in action.

* * * * *

Caught in these eddies of memory, Olga became aware that people were staring at her and that she was obstructing their passage through the narrow street. She stepped to one side and glanced up the stairway again. The day was one of those when a skittish wind was chasing clouds across the sky, allowing sudden bursts of sunlight to break through. The wall at the top of the flight was dark, but as she looked a ragged beam of brilliant white light flickered several times across it.

"Like the beating of an angel's wings," she murmured.

Reproving herself for whimsicality, Olga started to climb the steps. She went slowly, knowing that neither her eyes nor her balance were wholly reliable. The light on the wall ahead continued to flare and flicker. Three minutes later, for the first time ever, she rounded the bend and saw what was there. The illuminated wall was part of a derelict cottage but where it ended so did the path. Facing her in this cul-de-sac was a high brick wall inset with an arched doorway. The solid wooden door was ajar, swinging on its hinges, letting the sunlight through in an irregular rhythm.

Olga pushed the door wide open. She had not expected a witch, of course. Not now! She had supposed the door would lead on to a street. But, astonishing in its unexpectedness, stretching before her in all directions was a garden. It looked overgrown (but then it *was* May, when many gardens threaten to turn into jungles) and she sensed at once that it was not abandoned. The apple tree above her head was a froth of pink and white blossom. Birds piped and whistled all around her and in a lower register she could hear the steady humming of bees. Fragrance hung on the air, shed from old-fashioned pink roses tumbling over a broken wall, from a wisteria climbing through the naked branches of a stricken tree and from the thyme she crushed underfoot as she followed a cobbled path deeper into the garden.

She crossed a clearing, where bushes clipped into the shape of mythical green beasts seemed to watch her warily.

Through the trees now she could see a slate roof, twisted chimneys and the flash of light on latticed windows. From the same direction came the sound of human music, a ripple of notes played on a flute.

Drawn on by wonder and curiosity, Olga was startled by a rustling in the shrubbery beside her as a little girl came crawling out of the undergrowth. Seeing Olga, the child sprang to her feet. She was about ten years old, small and skinny. Leaves were caught in her spiky black hair and her yellow dress was splotched with mud.

"Hi!" she said.

Before Olga could respond, someone called from the house.

"Alannah! Alannah! Where are you? You haven't finished your music practice!"

"I was stalking a unicorn," shouted the girl. "But I've found a strange old woman instead!"

There were a few moments of silence while Olga adjusted to this description of herself and the girl picked the leaves out of her hair. Then there was the sound of thudding feet and a boy appeared at the end of the path. Ahead of him bounded a huge, shaggy, lion-like dog. The animal reached Olga and stopped. To her relief it neither barked nor leapt on her but simply stood regarding her calmly out of its amber eyes. The boy also stopped.

"Who are *you*," he asked gruffly, "and how did you get in the garden? Is the bloody gate open again?"

The girl frowned and shushed him. "Don't be so rude, Josh," she said. "She's probably one of Mummy's old ladies. And you know you should always be polite to the elderly."

The quaintness of her reproof made Olga laugh. The boy, rosy-cheeked and handsome, was bare-chested, his long shorts drawn in around his waist with a snake-headed belt. When Olga said nothing, both children stared silently at her, waiting. The dog whined and slumped down, resting his head on his paws.

"I'm sorry," she said at last. "The bloody gate *was* open, and I'm afraid I couldn't resist the temptation to see what was beyond it."

"Well, it's private," said Josh.

"It's very unexpected. And very beautiful."

"Yes," agreed the girl. "It's a secret garden. And it's very old. It was made by our Great-Grandmama."

Was she a witch, by any chance? Olga wanted to ask. But the boy was scowling at his sister. "Come on Alannah," he urged, "you've got to finish practising. And you shouldn't be talking to *strangers*. I'll see her out."

Alannah ignored him. Prompted by some spirit of politeness she asked Olga if she wanted to sit down.

"No, thank you. I was on my way back to my friends' house. I must go. But thank you for welcoming me to your garden."

"That's OK." Mollified, perhaps, by her thanks, Josh went on, "I'll come and lock the gate after you. Mum's always nervous of intruders getting in . . ."

"But surely that's not very likely? Why would anybody bother to climb a broken-down flight of steps that appear to lead to nowhere?"

"Well, *you* did," said the boy, "and they do lead somewhere. They lead to here."

"People call them the Stairway to Heaven," said Alannah.

"Yes. As a matter of fact, I knew that."

Olga found herself telling them how she had first discovered the steps. She said nothing about the witch, only that she had found the darkness of the stairway scary. "But I was very young – younger even than you are now," she concluded. Josh looked sceptical, as if he doubted such a thing were possible. Alannah, however, looked thoughtful.

"If it was during the war," she said, "it must have been when Great-Grandmama lived here."

The dog stood up, nuzzled Olga's hand and set off towards the distant gate. "I think he's dropping a hint I should go," she smiled.

"He's a *she*," said the girl, "and she's the ancestor of Great-Grandmama's dog."

The boy snorted. "Descendant!" he corrected her.

Alannah shrugged. "What's your name?" she asked Olga. "You didn't introduce yourself, you know. Visitors should always introduce themselves."

Olga offered her hand. "I'm Olga," she said.

The girl's reaction shocked her. Instead of taking her hand, Alannah started to jump up and down. "Hey, Josh," she shouted after her brother, who had set off to follow the dog. "Her name is Olga! It's Olga, Olga, OLGA!"

The dog came padding back and for a moment, Olga thought the animal's name must be Olga, too. But Josh also turned and came back. "So what?" he growled, but then, as if light were dawning, he said, "Oh, *Olga*! Are you sure?"

The children seemed galvanised now by some strange spell of excitement. They skipped around her, edging her nearer to the house, plying her with questions, squealing when she apparently got the answers right.

"It is! It is!" cried the girl. "It's *our* Olga! It's magic!"

Utterly bewildered, Olga stared across the lawn where she now stood. Fifty yards away was a handsome Jacobean house, its weathered red-brick front masked by the tender new growth of a Virginia creeper. A French window stood open onto the terrace. Before she could ask what all the fuss was about, the children both streaked away, the dog at their heels. Calling for their mother, they dashed across lawn and terrace and disappeared inside.

In the late afternoon sun, Olga sat on the veranda of her friends' house, where she was staying. Her usually tidy hair was all awry, straying wisps feathering her face and neck in the evening breeze. Her eyes were reddened and her hands still unsteady as she read, for the umpteenth time, the letter they held.

"*My dearest Olga,*" it began.

The ink was faded and the edges of the paper browned as if scorched by time. For seventy years the letter had lain in the workbox of a witch – a *mythical* witch – who in reality had been the great-grandmother of Josh and Alannah, and who, apparently, had always hoped that one day Olga would return and retrieve it.

"My grandmother always believed you would come," the children's mother had said. "She found this letter on the steps where you must have dropped it. But with no address, no clue other than your first name, she had no way of finding you. And it was such a moving letter, it so clearly would be precious, that we have kept it ever since."

"More precious than she could ever have guessed," Olga had said. "It was my father's last letter to me – although I did not know that then, of course. I had taken it out of its envelope and slipped it into my satchel to read again at school that day."

Once more she scanned the three flimsy pages of large, printed writing that had been intended for her six-year-old eyes. There were little jokes, simple anecdotes about her father's companions and precise, even poetic, descriptions of the desert landscape and the desert weather. Out of them, out of the past (in which his other letters had long ago been lost) her father's unique voice rang clearly down to her. Carefully she read the last paragraph.

"Sweetheart," he had written,

> *It isn't always easy to be brave. Everyone is frightened sometimes. For me, when I was little, it was the monster under my bed. For you it's the witch at the top of the Stairway to Heaven. But one day we'll be together again and hand in hand we will climb those steps, and perhaps at the top, instead of a witch, we will find an angel.*

"Which," thought Olga as she folded and then kissed the letter, "is exactly what I *did* find."

A WORLD OF TREES

Only when the last tree has died, the last river has been poisoned and the last fish has been caught, will we realise that we cannot eat money.

Cree Proverb

Deryn stood at the window and stared out at the ravaged world, the only world he knew, the only world that anyone alive now knew: the world of the Aftermath.

Sorrow engulfed him. How could they have let it happen, those long-ago generations of his own kind who had brought about the Great Catastrophe? He knew the stories only too well: how in the three centuries preceding the final holocaust they had mortally wounded the earth; how they had robbed the soil of its fertility, the air of its purity and the seas of their prodigality; how, for power and profit, they had destroyed the planet's finely tuned balances and, in the end, its ability to heal itself, and how, by the time they realised the extent and enormity of the problems they had created, it had been too late.

His mother had once told him that Deryn, the name she had chosen for him, meant 'bird' in her language. She had never seen a bird, nor heard one, but she gave him that name because her people were said to have been great singers and in all their legends birds were celebrated for their singing. Apart from the scrawny chickens that scratched endlessly and fruitlessly at the blighted soil in the patch of ground behind his cottage, Deryn had never seen a bird either. The squawking of the poultry, he thought, was even worse than his own singing!

He closed his eyes and tried to imagine the valley as it must have been in the Pre-Catastrophe era. Based on the pictures he had been shown and the stories he had been told, he saw a world of trees: trees whose leaves emerged every spring in countless varieties of shape and shades of green; trees whose branches gave shelter to choirs of birds which sang or piped or whistled and filled the valley with music; trees whose flowers scented the air and whose fruits fed millions of creatures from the lowliest of bugs to the mightiest of kings, and trees whose wood had built this cottage and supplied the people of that time with the wherewithal to furnish it – and with fuel to keep it warm in winter.

Unable to sustain these images in his head, Deryn's eyes flicked open. Today the everlasting clouds hung very low, shrouding the peaks and darkening the air over the brown and wasted hills. Their flanks were almost bare, only spiked here and there with the broken and decaying stumps of what had once been a forest. Lower down he could see the tiny plots where the last survivors around him still struggled to grow enough cereal to produce a small sackful of grain each year, to cultivate a few sickly vegetables or to nurture a sapling apple tree they hoped might reach the height of a man before succumbing to the poisoned air, the corrupted earth and the relentless rain.

Leaving the window, Deryn sank into his chair beside the embers of the fire lit by his grandson. When not foraging for food the boy spent hours gleaning the foothills for the scanty remains of dead timber to keep it going. Nowadays, age and weariness, hunger and weakness, penned Deryn himself indoors. Only his mind could escape and wander freely and, thinking of his grandson (who had never seen, who never *would* see, a full-grown tree), Deryn recalled the day he was taken by his own grandfather to see the last living tree in the country.

They had walked many miles before they joined a swelling throng of people who were all heading in the same direction. There had been some chatter and a few songs, but the crowd was largely silent as they approached the knoll on which the tree stood. The thing he remembered seeing first (way above the heads of the people labouring to climb the hill) was a dense green cloud that seemed to float against the grey sky behind it. He had tugged his hand free of his grandfather's gnarled fingers and squeezed his way through the crush until he stood only twenty paces from the iron fence that encircled the tree.

Oh, the wonder of it!

The tree's trunk soared into the sky, its branches arching out and up until trying to follow them with his eyes made Deryn feel dizzy. A slight breeze was moving through them, making them murmur softly and shaking their green leaves, which rustled with a sound like whispered laughter. Entranced, he had moved closer until he could read the notice fixed on the fence.

"This is the last living tree," it said, *"in the world."*

Behind the barrier two burly men were pacing to and fro. They wore uniforms on which the words

GUARDIAN OF THE TREE

were printed in large black letters, and were struggling to control a couple of great dogs that had lunged towards Deryn, straining at their leashes, their fangs bared in a snarl.

"Get away," shouted one of the men. "They don't like 'ee touchin' the fence!"

Deryn had shrunk back into the crowd. The wind was beginning to strengthen, sighing through the branches of the tree and whipping the leaves into a frenzy. A long answering sigh rose from the people and some of them, he saw, were weeping. A few leaves were torn free and as they flickered down a small girl standing beside him had captured one and pressed it to her cheek.

"Green," she had murmured. "Green . . ."

Rain had started to fall, pattering on the leaves before turning rapidly into a deluge that quickly soaked through Deryn's flimsy jerkin.

"Come," said his grandfather, hobbling towards him as the crowd began to disperse. "We must go. But at least we've seen the tree. Now you must hold it in your head so that you can describe it to *your* grandchildren."

"No," Deryn had said. "Words could never explain the miracle of it. I shall do as you've done and bring them to see it."

The old man had shaken his head. "The tree is dying," he said. "Even before your children are grown it will cease to exist."

Deryn had cried then, but for forty years, while his bones warped, his back became stooped and his teeth decayed away, he had held the tree in his head. He had outlived most of his neighbours in the valley and all of his children. Wryly he thought that maybe the time had come when *he* could be fenced about and protected by ferocious dogs, with a notice beside him that said, "*This is the last man on earth to have seen a living tree.*"

These days he spent many hours in sleep and sometimes the tree he had seen appeared to him in his dreams. Sometimes, too, it was multiplied a thousand times until it became a whole world of trees where the light was shadowed with green and the ground splashed with gold by sunlight filtering through their canopy. In these dreams he could hear again the murmur of boughs above him, the whispered conversation of leaves – and beneath his feet he could feel the deep silence of the roots.

And *once*, from somewhere in the hidden depths of that living, breathing, green world, he had caught a sound he had never heard in his waking world, a sound that had woken him, weeping for the loss of it.

A brief arpeggio of pure, clear, piping notes. The exquisite song of a bird . . .

MISSING

DAFI

said the poster in large letters, and beneath that,

MISSING!

Jemima, dreaming her way along the street as usual, stopped in her tracks. She stared at the paper pinned to the lamp-post and was struck as if by a lightning bolt. A passer-by glanced at her and hesitated, and then stopped, came back a step and spoke to her.

"Are you all right?" he asked.

"I'm fine," Jemima assured him. "It's just – I've suddenly remembered something."

The stranger's expression of concern changed to one of amusement. "Ah!" he said. "I see." His smile held a hint of sympathy and a hint of complicity. He was elderly (but not yet as ancient as herself) and would know about the game of hide-and-seek that memory plays as one ages. But, of course, he did not 'see'. This, thought Jemima, was not that. Her own phrasing made her smile too, and with a genial word of farewell the man moved on.

She looked again at the poster. It was fluttering now in the little breeze that whispered among the yellowing leaves of the birch tree behind her. Its message and the picture of a malignant-looking black cat were faded by weeks of wind and weather, and she was surprised she had not noticed it before. Maybe it was because such pleadings were commonplace nowadays, she thought. Cats seemed to get lost for a pastime. Like others of its kind, the poster requested that people 'search in their sheds and garages' for a lost, loved pet.

Briefly, Jemima hoped that this one had been found, but the shock of recovering a memory that, as far as she knew, had lain buried (the word made her flinch) for over seventy years, made her legs feel weak. Above all she wanted to sit down and think, recall the details of its source and dig for the truth.

Ten minutes later, sitting in the small, warm café at the corner of Enderby Street, her shoes shucked off beneath the table, her good winter coat (worn for the first time today) padding the back of the hard chair, she took a sip of Mr. Patel's hot, strong tea and, closing her eyes, retreated into the distant past.

* * * * *

It was Maggie who was responsible, she thought. Her older cousin, Maggie. Tall, plump, blowsily blonde and sexy already at thirteen, Maggie had been staying with Jemima's family while her own mother was in hospital having her fifth baby. Jemima remembered that as an only child herself, she had envied Maggie her three younger sisters, although Maggie had seemed to find them a burden.

Here Jemima paused the reel of recollections that, to her astonishment, was now unwinding with great clarity in her head. Had her cousin, she wondered, been upset by the arrival of yet another sibling? Was that the reason for her revelation that day? Or was it merely carelessness? Did she know that in Jemima's home the story had never even been hinted at – that it was a skeleton closeted away in the deepest, darkest corner of the family's historical, emotional, and psychological cupboard?

"I'll never know the answer to that, I suppose," murmured Jemima taking a longer swig of tea before spreading a thick layer of salty butter on the first half of her scone.

The café was quiet. But in an hour's time, when the schools closed for the day, Jemima knew it would fill with chattering children and mothers battling to keep order amid noisy demands for ice cream, cake and orange juice.

"You OK, Miss Jem?" asked Mr. Patel as he wiped a nearby table just deserted by a young couple. "More tea? Another scone?"

She smiled mistily at him, her head still roaming another time and place. He was a nice man. Always called her Miss Jem, never having mastered the pronunciation of her Welsh surname, Prydderch, and too shy to settle for her first name only.

"A second scone would be lovely," she said. "But the teapot is still half full, thank you."

She watched people hurrying past as the first spots of a shower spattered the window, distorting her view of the row of small, shabby shops (all struggling to survive) on the opposite side of the road.

How different this Midlands town was from the Welsh village where she grew up! It, too, had been impoverished, but the terrace of farmworkers' cottages fronting the street where she and Maggie had walked that day all had doorsteps that were scrubbed and whitened daily, and scarlet or salmon-pink geraniums flourished in almost every window. Hand in hand the two girls had hurried along the narrow streets, heading into the open countryside, where Maggie said they were going to pick a bunch of wild flowers for Jemima's mother: honeysuckle from the hedgerows, buttercups and cornflowers and ragged robin from the grassy banks that sheltered the lanes.

As they left the last house behind and began to climb the hill, they had heard the church clock strike the hour.

"Four o'clock," Maggie said. "I wonder if Mam has had the babby yet? I hope to goodness it's a *boy* for a change!"

"You're lucky," said Jemima. At six she was still an only child (and would indeed remain so). "I've never had a brother *or* a sister, and I wouldn't care *what* it was."

Maggie had released her hand, stopped and looked down at her with a thoughtful expression in her blue eyes.

"Well," she said slowly. "You did have a brother once. Only they lost him, didn't they?"

Seventy-five years later, with Mr. Patel setting a fresh, warm scone in front of her (together with two pats of butter), the shock she had suffered at six years old rocked Jemima again.

How? How could she ever have forgotten that moment? She remembered now the utter bewilderment she had felt as she stared up at Maggie, aghast and disbelieving. A hundred questions had numbed her brain.

"Who?" she had said at last. "*Who* lost him?"

"Your Mam and Dad, of course," said Maggie.

"Where?" said Jemima. "Where? When? *How* did they lose him? Didn't they *look* for him?"

Alerted, perhaps, by these agonised questions and remembering – or realising – she had trespassed on forbidden ground, Maggie had laughed and then shrugged, grasped Jemima's hand again and tugged her onwards.

"He's been missing since long before you were born," she had said airily. "So what does it matter?"

Jemima recalled that, even at such a young age, she had been startled at such a callous response.

It mattered, thought the adult Jemima, as she wetted one finger and mopped up the last crumbs of her scone, because all through her childhood she had sensed an unexplained sorrow in her mother and an absence of something (a warmth, a spontaneity) in her father. And it also mattered because at that moment when Maggie told her an abyss opened up at her feet: an abyss created by this new knowledge that it was possible for a child to go missing; to be lost and never found again . . .

"Why aren't they *still* looking for him?" she had cried at the time.

She had stopped walking and started to weep. Through her tears she saw, on the barbed wire that separated the bank from the field above, half a dozen dead crows. They were hanging upside down, their eyes dulled or missing, their feathers bloody and bedraggled. The horror of it somehow mingled in her mind with her distress about her lost brother and, wrenching her hand out of Maggie's, she had started to run back down the hill. Maggie had chased after her.

"Oh, God," her cousin had said, as she caught and hugged her. "You don't understand, do you? Your Mam and Dad didn't lose your brother in the way you're thinking! And they don't need to *look* for him, *cariad*. They *know* where he is . . ."

* * * * *

Try as she might, Jemima, at eighty-one, could not remember what had happened after that. Had they gone on with their walk or had they returned home? She simply

220

could not recall. But thinking about it now she saw that it was not just Maggie's revelation that had upset and misled her. It was her own childish misunderstanding of her cousin's choice of words, 'lost' and 'missing'.

Something must have happened in the interval between *that* time and the moment, later on, when she had stood beside her mother in the village churchyard. Above them, she recollected, the church tower had loomed, and from behind it had radiated a dazzling fan of light from the setting sun,

"I'm so sorry, Jem," her mother was whispering. "I suppose we should have shown you long ago . . . this is where your brother is . . ."

She pointed to where, at their feet, a diminutive gravestone stood, overgrown with grass, speckled with grey and gold rosettes of lichen and engraved with words. Jemima was only just learning to read and many of the letters were masked by the lichen or blurred by thirteen years of weathering. Only the name, 'Dafi', was clear to her.

"What does it say?" she had asked.

"*Dafi Prydderch*," murmured her mother. "*Beloved son of Dafydd and Mari. Born 1925. Died 1930.*"

Her voice made an odd choking sound and she stopped.

"There's more," said Jemima, who could see the word '*missing*' and others beyond it.

"*Missing for ever in our lives,*" said Mam. "*Present for ever in our hearts.*"

She had gripped Jemima's hand so hard that it hurt and with the fingers of her other hand had brushed her cheek where tears glittered like jewels in the sun's brilliance.

* * * * *

"Miss Jem, Miss Jem!"

Mr. Patel's voice broke into the trance that held her. The sun was blazing into the café, transforming the raindrops on the window to shining prisms that flickered on the wall like stars.

"Are you all right, Miss Jem?" asked Mr. Patel, the concern in his voice making it gruff. "You were crying."

He handed her a clean paper napkin and she mopped her eyes. "I can't think why," she said. "Dafi would be ninety-three now – and dead anyway, I expect."

Mr. Patel, clearly baffled, made no response to this other than to pat her shoulder and assure her she could sit there for as long as she liked.

He probably thinks I'm getting battier by the day, she thought ruefully.

Without the accident that had killed him, would her brother, like her, have lived to a great age, grown battier and become a nuisance to himself and a concern to others?

Maggie was long dead, and since that fateful summer's day they had seen little of each other and had never spoken of the business of the lost boy. But Jemima was grateful to her now. If it had not been for Maggie, she might never have known she had a brother. Apart from that one visit to his grave, her parents had maintained their silence. Frozen in grief, guilt and regret, they never spoke of their son.

Years later it was her grandmother who told Jemima how, in a moment of inattention (quarrelling about some trivial matter), they had both let go of his hand in a busy street and he had run straight out into the path of a car. It was her grandmother, too, who had given Jemima the only photograph they had of Dafi and over the years had passed on some of his funny sayings; told her stories about his adventures, described how he had frequently got into trouble for climbing trees, for digging up their father's newly-planted vegetables and for calling his mother by her first name, and how once he had made biscuits (with her help) that were so iron-hard that they broke one of her teeth . . .

Jemima had treasured these second-hand memories and had even passed them on to her own son, Dafydd (born out of wedlock – oh dear! – when she was almost past childbearing age). She had never forgotten about her brother. What she *had* forgotten, though, was the occasion (fortuitously returned to her today) on which she first discovered he had existed.

Outside, she could hear children whooping and laughing, their feet scuttering along the pavement as they raced each other for the café. Jemima stood up, fished in her purse for the correct change, and handed it to Mr. Patel as he stood watching the children through the window.

"Do you believe in our immortality, Mr. Patel?" she asked him.

He looked startled, challenged. "Well, now, Miss Jem," he said. "Immortality? Now that's a big question! Perhaps if we have created some great work . . . but . . ."

She laughed. "Or perhaps if we stay in the memories of those who have loved us?" she ventured. "In the stories they tell of us – the stories they pass down through the generations? Perhaps in that way a little bit of us survives . . ."

"Sure, Miss Jem," he said. "Sure."

The children were clustering now at the door and, taking her arm, he waved them away as he gently ushered her out. She smiled at him and then at the children who were jostling each other . . . impatient to get in . . . impatient to get on with their lives . . .

THE SHED

The storm, threatening all afternoon, broke just as Jenny reached the bottom of the garden. She had ventured down through the wilderness to pick the last of the raspberries, but as she reached in among the drooping leaves for the fruit, lightning cracked the sky above the mountain. Simultaneously, thunder detonated overhead and rain sluiced down, filling the bowl she carried in seconds and soaking her to the bone.

With a protesting cry she brushed through the dripping canes, shoved at the door of the old potting shed and stumbled inside. Here the gloom deepened to utter darkness, the one window so masked with ivy that it admitted no light at all. Gradually her eyes adjusted. No-one had entered here since Gryff's death five years before. Cobwebs, heavy with dust, draped over rusting garden tools, leaning towers of empty plant pots, a clutter of watering cans and her grandfather's ancient wooden wheelbarrow. In the far corner where the floor had crumbled away a white fungus spread like curds of cheese and everything smelled of damp earth, death and decay. As rain pounded the roof and thunder crashed again, Jenny imagined she heard Gryff's voice.

"Sorry, *cariad*," he was saying, "I should have got rid of all this stuff long ago. But whenever I threw *anything* out you can bet I found a use for it the very next day!"

Fifty years ago, barely a year after their marriage, she and Gryff had moved into her grandfather's house. The old man's failing health meant that the garden had been long neglected and it took years to restore it. Between the half-acre vegetable patch and what Gryff laughingly called 'the pleasure garden' they had installed a handsome modern workshop, so that this shed, tucked under the boundary hedge, had become merely a storehouse for things they no longer used. Left to fall apart, it had also served as Gryff's hideaway, his refuge from the pressures of teaching, from the demands of the family, even on occasion from Jenny herself. Beneath the smells of mould and creosote, of rotting wood and dried-up vegetation, Jenny thought she could detect, faint and far away, the fragrance of his tobacco smoke.

Swept by a wave of sorrow, she started to sort through the junk on the bench under the window: an old biscuit tin full of assorted nails and screws; a box of earthenware shards; another of dog-eared seed catalogues; a sieve for sifting soil for seedbeds . . .

She winced at this accidental alliteration but thought how much Gryff would have enjoyed it. She was repeating it aloud when a sudden gust of wind thrashed the ivy against the glass and a ray of light, filtering through the tossing leaves, glinted on something at the back of the bench.

Drawing it towards her, Jenny saw that it was a brass cauldron, grey with verdigris except for one tiny patch the light had picked out. At once she remembered how it had stood in her grandfather's kitchen window and how, under her care, the Christmas cactus it contained had flourished for years after he died. Then one of the children (Idris probably!) had swept it off the ledge in some wild game, smashing the plant and damaging the pot. Jenny smiled and dabbled her hand in what remained of the compost inside it. Dried to the consistency of ash, it trickled away through her fingers, leaving something small and solid on her palm.

Slowly she sank into the wheelbarrow behind her. The object in her hand was a silver ring, its metal (probably not silver at all!) tarnished to black. But the claw at its apex still held the moss green stone that Gryff had likened to the colour of her eyes.

As she gazed at it she saw, not the ring, but the market where, merely a week after they had first met, she and Gryff had wandered hand in hand. How old had they been? Fourteen? Fifteen? For three years, to avoid parental scrutiny, she had worn the ring he'd bought her there on a silken thread around her neck, transferring it to her middle finger only when they became officially engaged with a 'proper' ring. Later, as her hands enlarged, she had moved it to her little finger. And then she had lost it.

Distraught, she had turned the whole house upside down until Gryff had protested, "Come on, Jenny, love! It's not worth the grief! It was cheap trash. We'll go out tomorrow and I'll buy you another one. A better one!"

But nothing could replace it. Nothing could bring back the thrill, the joy, the *ecstasy* of that moment when they had stood side by side beneath the flapping awning of a market stall and he had slipped it onto her finger. And now, here it was, restored to her again, the ring and the thrill together!

Stiffly she climbed out of the barrow as another little spatter of rain struck the window. But the storm had receded, the thunder grumbling now at a distance. Pushing open the shed door and stepping outside, Jenny saw over the mountain that the clouds had parted and that the sun, just about to set, had come out and was transforming all the water droplets around her to sparks of golden light.

THE LOCK-KEEPER'S COTTAGE

I   *THE REED BEDS*

He crouched in what appeared to him to be a forest of coarse grass. His heart was beating so fast that it seemed his whole body throbbed and although his ears were straining to catch any sound of pursuit, all he could hear above its pounding was the blare of a train's siren in the distance and closer to, the squawking of some unknown night-bird.

Slowly his panic subsided and he became aware of other sounds, other discomforts: the sucking of water trapped in mud when he tried to shift his feet, the brittle rasping of the stalks around him, the damp cold, the utter darkness. He could not even see the lights of the village from which he had just fled and the sky was too overcast for any stars to be visible.

Still clutched in his hand was the greasy packet of fish and chips, cold now, that he had snatched from the woman outside the shop. He began to eat the food, but the woman's shrieks still rang in his head, mingling queasily there with his shame and guilt, so that starving as he was (for he had eaten nothing since he came out of the sea) he found it almost impossible to swallow.

When, at last, the final tasteless morsel had been forced down, he stood up. His cramped muscles ached and the clogging mud released him reluctantly. Here in this wilderness there was nothing to guide him. He yearned for his father (Oh, where was his father?), for his skill in finding ways through the hostile world, for his fierce love that would not let Ishmael fail, for the reassuring sound of his voice and for the feel of his strong, square hand around his own.

Tears squeezed from his eyes as he saw again the last wave crashing over the boat and felt the sickening swing as the frail vessel veered and juddered before upending and flinging everyone on board into the ocean. He groaned and covered his ears but could not shut out the remembered sound of their cries, the screaming and splashing and gasping as they struggled to stay afloat. In all the noise and confusion and darkness he had not been able to find his father before the angry waves, stronger by far than his own strength, had swept him away.

* * * * *

Ishmael had no idea how long he had lain unconscious on the beach where the sea had cast him up. He had been roused by the discomfort of a sharp stone pressing into his cheek and moments later had staggered out on to a nearby road that led him, after several kilometres, to the village where he had stolen the food. Since fleeing from there, it seemed to him he had been walking aimlessly through an eternal night. His thoughts were frozen in his head and he remembered only that the sea had taken his father – and that he, Ishmael, had failed him, had abandoned him to its clutches.

The sky had stayed overcast, the darkness unrelieved by any light. The waterlogged landscape around him was invisible but he was aware of sometimes struggling through whispering reed beds and sometimes walking across bare, unfenced areas of rough pasture. A thin, cold rain had started to fall and in the clouded darkness he occasionally tumbled into a narrow drainage ditch and had to wade through icy, weed-choked water. Once or twice he came upon a rickety bridge to cross and several times he stumbled upon a track made by some wild animal and followed it until it petered out in more reed beds or marshland.

By the time he caught sight of distant lights glimmering through the mist his anorak, which had started to dry out on the road, was drenched again. His sweater and jeans clung coldly to his flesh and his backpack, empty of almost everything except water, weighed heavily on his shoulders. The rain began to ease, however, and as he drew nearer the lights became clearer and he could tell by the spread of them that they marked some kind of settlement.

Silhouetted against the sky to his right he could see a small knoll topped by a few bare trees and skirting this he plunged into yet another reed bed. The rushes were as tall as he was, so it was not until he emerged from them that he saw the wide canal that cut him off from the land ahead where the lights still shone. With an anguished cry, knowing he had neither the strength to swim across it nor to walk any farther, he dropped to his knees and crawled along the dusty path alongside it.

The first hint of daylight was beginning to streak the sky over the sea, touching with gold the ragged edges of the clouds on the horizon. Glancing up, Ishmael saw the gold reflected in the steel struts of a bridge only a few metres away. He struggled to stand upright, and with hope giving him a brief renewal of energy he staggered on and by clinging to the handrail of the bridge, dragged himself across it.

On the far side of the canal there were yet more reeds, their flower heads rustling in the dawn breeze. As he plunged in among them roosting birds fussed at his intrusion but wearily he pressed on until, at last, the reed beds came to an end and he stepped clear. The rising sun flashed on another stretch of water, only five paces from where he stood, and he saw that between him and the settlement which was his goal there flowed a broad and swiftly-moving river.

II   THE HULK

To the people of the town the wrecked vessel that lay locked in the mud and besieged by reeds on the far side of the river was known as The Old Hulk. Possibly this was because it reminded them of the prison ship from which the convict, Magwitch, escapes at the beginning of *Great Expectations*. This hulk, however, had never held a prisoner. It was merely an old pleasure craft that once had ferried tourists down the estuary to the seaside town at the river's mouth. One long-ago night when a ferocious sou'westerly gale had coincided with a flood tide, the boat had been wrenched from its moorings and, battered by the wind and broken by the waves, had been swept upriver and dumped on the marshy riverbank, where it had now lain for most of a century.

Throughout that time it had resisted all further attempts of wind and waves to shift it. Tilted on its side, its bows resting in the reed beds, its stern washed twice daily by the tide, it had quietly rotted away. As it did not disrupt traffic on the river it was left there undisturbed while its timbers shrank and greened with weed and its superstructure grew ever more skeletal and picturesque. It was the haunt of gulls and rats and sanctuary to a thousand unseen nibbling, gnawing creatures that would eventually reduce it to dust. It had become part of the landscape, unregarded by all except perhaps for an occasional artist or questing marine biologist.

It was in this ghost of a boat that Ishmael found refuge. He crawled through a great rent in the landward side of the hull and collapsed amid the debris of rat droppings, rusting shards of ironwork, tide-borne pebbles and broken rushes that littered the floor. For two days he slept, afflicted by a mild fever and drifting in and out of consciousness. Remembering, forgetting, dreaming . . .

In his short waking periods he was aware of hunger and, more painfully, of thirst. Towards the end of the first day, he discovered that the recent rain, dripping through a hole in the decking above him, had collected in a puddle on a rag of tarpaulin beside him. He raised his head and lapped at it like a dog. The hunger he could endure. It had been his frequent companion on the journey with his father, the journey that had brought them across years and across continents before delivering him alone on the shores of the place that Izak had been so devotedly determined to reach.

"Why England?" Ishmael had asked, for some of the places where they had rested on their travels had seemed to him to be good places, places he would have been happy to stay. "What is it about England?"

"Because I believe," said Izak, "that in an increasingly uncivilised world England remains a civilised place. Its system of government is tainted but not yet totally corrupted by the ugly power of money. Its long-established laws are respected because they are largely just and – more importantly – are justly practised. It is free of war and famine, still tolerant of strangers, and offers great possibilities for those who live according to those laws and are willing to work."

He had paused there and then, with a characteristic twinkle in his dark eyes, had added, "Besides – they speak English there!"

Ishmael had not understood all of this because at the time his father himself had been speaking in English. He was teaching Ishmael the language, insisting on both of them practising it for hours each day as they travelled across deserts, trudged through cities, or tramped among mountains. When they began these lessons Ishmael had been ten years old. Now he was fourteen and his command of his father's chosen language was better but still far from fluent.

Quite recently, after getting tangled up with grammar and syntax and deciding the language was impossible he had sulkily challenged his father.

"Why do I have to learn English?" he had asked. "It's too difficult. And we may never get to England anyway!"

"Ha!" said Izak. His eyes had glinted with fervour and he had buffeted his son lightly on the shoulder. "Of course we will get there! And when we do, if you don't speak the language you will be isolated, excluded – and remain an alien all your life. In any case, English is a world language, and above all else we must aim to be citizens of the world."

Remembering these conversations brought his father's image briefly but vividly into Ishmael's head. From long exposure to the sun and wind Izak's face had been deeply lined and almost black. When he laughed (as he often did) Ishmael could see the gaps in his lower jaw from where two teeth had been extracted by an itinerant dentist. His beard was turning grey, but his hair was still dark and thick and hung almost to his waist. When he spoke, his voice was deep and eloquent: it commanded attention, especially when he was reading from one of his favourite texts.

"I love English!" he had once said, setting his book aside in order to clean his spectacles with the hem of his shirt. "Its vocabulary is so huge – a vast hotch-potch of words begged, borrowed and stolen from other lang-uages. This wealth of words makes it easier to achieve accuracy, precision and nuance when trying to pin down meaning. It is also, essentially, a poetic language, ranging easily from the abstract to the concrete and turning constantly to metaphor." He had replaced his glasses and smiled at Ishmael. "After all," he said, "it is the language of Shakespeare!"

Though bored with much of this, Ishmael had listened patiently. His father's passion for Shakespeare was part of his passion for literature. Before Izak had taken up the science he taught at the university (until war had sent both it and him packing), it had been the main focus of his study. But the boy preferred it when his father's talk was of his mother. She had been killed soon after Ishmael was born and he had no memories of her other than those contained in Izak's stories.

"She was beautiful," he would say, "as well as witty and wise. And in spite of the horrors, the suffering she experienced, she had such *zest* for life . . ."

At this his eyes would blur with tears and he would be silent, brooding for many minutes before he could resume. The small black and white photograph of his wife he carried had first faded and finally disintegrated altogether from frequent handling. When her image had disappeared entirely, they buried the scrap of paper that had held it beneath a cherry tree crowned with white blossom.

"Because," said Izak, "cherries were a fruit that she particularly loved."

* * * * *

When, on the third day, Ishmael woke up properly, weak but free from fever, his arrival in this bleak refuge was already a dim memory. All he could recall was the flat wilderness of reeds, mud and water through which he had toiled, the winking lights that had guided him through the dark and his despair when in the dawn light he saw they were out of reach, on the far side of the turbulent river that was rushing past his feet.

He sat up. His head ached, all his limbs felt stiff and sore and his clothes were still clammily damp. A little breeze, scurrying up the river, whistled through the gaps in the boat's planking and made him shiver. Except for the raucous squabbling of the gulls above and the sound of some small animal scrabbling in the litter at the far end of the cabin, he could hear nothing.

Somehow, although his legs felt scarcely able to support him, he struggled to his feet. He had no idea of the time but it was daylight and in spite of the gloom in the hold he was able to see that the space he was in ran almost the full length of the boat. Cobwebs, clogged with ancient dust, sagged from the joists supporting the upper deck and through a jagged hole in the floor the muddy riverbed was visible. This hole he had already used as a toilet and as he did so again he noticed the mud was streaked with seaweed and brown froth was beginning to lap over it where the water level was rising. The river, he realised, must be tidal.

Above his head the skeletal remains of a staircase rose to the upper deck and, carefully working his way up the broken treads, he found himself in an airy open cabin beneath a roof that was mostly intact. From here he could clearly see the settlement on the far bank.

Directly opposite him, a few small boats were moored close to a road that ran along the waterfront. The road was backed by an enormously high wall and behind it a church tower showed black against the pale sky. Beneath the parapet of the tower a clock face marked a time Ishmael could not see and above it a flag flapped, the white ship on its blue ground seeming to buck and toss as the wind played with it.

To the left of this road a cluster of ancient buildings stood shoulder to shoulder, some with their foundations actually in the water; and to the right of it a forest of masts, like skinny branchless trees, rose from what he thought must be a boatyard. Beyond that, the river widened and there were larger buildings, warehouses he decided, or possibly modern apartment blocks.

In the distance he could hear the muffled roar of heavy traffic and from the town itself the sound of voices raised in a shouted conversation. He stood for a while, watching the river as the incoming tide swept steadily upstream until, carried on the breeze, the metallic repetitions of the church clock told him it was ten o'clock.

* * * * *

Ishmael left the hulk by the way he had entered it, on the landward side, and forging his way through the head-high rushes he returned to the canal. While still hidden in the reeds he checked there was no one about before he crossed the bridge, turned left and began to walk along the towpath. The sun had come out and although there was little warmth in it, together with the breeze it began to dry his clothes.

His sweater was worn thin, his anorak had no lining and in spite of the sun he was cold as well as nauseous from hunger. He wondered why his father would choose to come to such a cold, grey wilderness as England seemed to be when his speciality was the study of world climates! But now that he was fully awake, thinking about his father was dangerous (the loss of him, the longing for him) and by looking about him and taking note of the landscape he steered his thoughts away.

The canal towpath lay along the top of a bank from where he could see the marsh he had crossed nights ago. Sheep and a few cattle were grazing there but there was no sign of a farm or cottage where he might beg the food he desperately needed. Against distant hills a jagged line of rooftops marked the village he had fled from but even had he felt brave enough to return there it was too far for him to reach. His head was fuzzy and his legs felt as if they lacked bones and might give way at any minute.

He stopped for a moment to rest. Although very close, the river was not visible from here and the canal stretched in a straight line to the horizon. The path beside it was fringed with stunted trees all entwined with brambles and as he moved on he found a few shrivelled berries clinging to their leafless stems. Later he passed a bench where walkers could rest and beneath it he found a discarded package containing a half-eaten sandwich. Retching at the stale taste and soggy texture, he nevertheless devoured it and plodded on. Not long afterwards he spotted a thin column of smoke drifting into the sky ahead of him and moments later a solitary house came into sight.

Close to the house the canal entered a deep lock spanned by a narrow bridge and, turning aside from the path, Ishmael crossed it. He found himself on a paved terrace where chairs, tables and wooden tubs, scruffy with the withered remains of summer geraniums, were randomly scattered. A half-empty bottle of beer stood on a wall and from within the house the smell of roasting meat filled the air. Above the open door, an inn sign creaked to and fro in the strengthening, sea-scented breeze and it took Ishmael a few moments to work out the unfamiliar letters that spelled its name.

World's End, it said.

* * * * *

The dog came out of nowhere. A big, shaggy, lollopy sort of dog, it barked madly as it ran at Ishmael, before leaping up and almost bowling him over. A lifetime's experience of aggressive dogs made him nervous and he cowered back. The dog came in again, but from somewhere a voice yelled, "Dingbat! Lay off. Come here, you stupid animal!"

The dog hesitated and retreated a little way but continued to bark. Behind it, strolling round the corner of the pub, a boy of about Ishmael's age appeared.

"Hi!" he said, giving the dog a light slap on the rump but looking at Ishmael. "That was just Dingbat's way of saying hello. He won't hurt you."

Ishmael neither moved nor spoke. Dog and boy stood staring intently at him as he took in the fact that the boy was carrying a paper plate loaded with food: a beef-burger surrounded by a heap of salad. His mouth filled with bitter water and his stomach cramped.

"You OK?" asked the boy, taking a bite out of the burger. "You look a bit . . . that is . . . my Dad would say you look as though you've been dragged through a hedge backwards!" There was a glint of amusement in his blue eyes. His pale yellow hair was cropped short and stood up in a tuft on his crown. "Did you come with the ferry people?"

"The fairy people?"

Ishmael was confused and his voice, not used for several days, was hoarse and faint. The boy looked startled. He frowned and moved closer, the dog watchful at his heels.

"The ferry," he repeated. "Did you come with the others on the boat? Or did you walk here?"

"Walk," croaked Ishmael. "I walk on path by canal."

His eyes were fixed on the food. He wondered if he could beg a bite or two from the boy. In their long travels, he and Izak had occasionally been forced to beg for food, although their pride had always rebelled and they had never got used to it. Before he could find the words he needed, however, the boy said, "Your accent's weird! You're not from round here, are you?"

"No," agreed Ishmael. "I from . . . from far away . . ."

"Are you English?"

"Not yet," said Ishmael, instinctively clinging to his father's determination, his confidence, that they would eventually *be* English. Instantly he regretted those words, fearful that the boy would at once realise he had no right to be here, and would rush off to fetch some person in authority who would arrest him.

But the boy just laughed. He finished the burger, gave a tit-bit of meat to the dog and set his plate down on the nearest table.

"Can't stand that rabbit food," he said. "You've been staring at it as if you were a starving rabbit yourself. If you want it, you're welcome."

Then, with another sharp glance at Ishmael, he turned on his heel and walked away.

* * * * *

Moonlight seeped through the cracks in the boat's hull where the boards had shrunk apart. The angle of the wreck, tipped on to its left side, meant that Ishmael kept slithering off the bed he had made from a sheaf of rushes cut with his pocket-knife. He slept fitfully, his sleep haunted by dreams of his father.

When at last he woke it was still dark but the clock on the tower was striking seven. He dragged his backpack from where it had cushioned his head and felt around inside it for the remains of the food he had filched from the bins in the backyard at World's End. The boy's salad had scarcely touched his craving for food, but in the bins he had found half-eaten buns, discarded crusts, chicken bones with rags of meat still attached, morsels of other meat, scraps of wilted salad and one whole fried egg, its yolk rubbery, its frilled edges burnt and crisp. This, and some of the bread, he had saved for his breakfast.

The food was foul but it gave him a little energy and as the sun rose he hauled himself out of the dank smelly hold and, avoiding rotting planks and splintery holes, made his way on to the upper deck. He knew now that when the tide was full it reached as far as the wreck, gurgling in and out of the gaps in its lower structure and lisping among the reeds. This morning it was out and the river had dwindled to a narrow channel surrounded by acres of mud. The low sun glared on its shining brown surface glossing it with iridescent patches of purple, green and blue.

Ishmael crawled into the bows, from where he could see upriver. In the distance a great modern road bridge straddled the whole valley but where the town thinned out he could see fields and yet more reed beds. One or two sailing boats stood on their keels in the mud and a row of upturned dinghies, drawn up on the field edge, lay there like giant stranded beetles.

Shaken with fear at the thought of ever going out on the water again in a boat, he saw that to reach the town (where he might find food as well as a way out into the wider spaces of England) he would need one; but as far as he could see there were no boats moored on his side of the river. For a few moments he contemplated trying to walk across, but if he did that he would be totally exposed to the eyes of the town. In any case the mud was probably deep and treacherous, and might suck him down and drown him in its choking depths.

With a shudder he turned away, but to honour his father's dreams and his steadfast, lifelong pursuit of them, Ishmael knew he *had* to move on.

"We must never give up," Izak had said. "This one and only life we have is far too precious to waste in idleness or hopelessness, in accepting the unacceptable. Settling for mere survival cannot be enough. If necessary, we must go to the ends of the earth to find and fulfil our own chosen purpose in life."

The remembered words, encapsulating as they did Izak's idealism and his dreams, caught Ishmael unawares. Grief surged through him, bringing with it an overwhelming sense of loneliness. There was nowhere – nowhere in England, nowhere in all the lands he had traversed, nowhere *in the whole wide world* – where anyone existed who knew and loved him.

Once, when he had been much younger, he had said to his father how much he hated the people who had driven them out, who were persecuting them and devastating their country. Izak had enfolded him in his arms but shaken his head.

"On no account give hatred any space in your heart, my son," he had said. "Hatred is corrosive. Hatred diminishes us. It is love that makes us grow . . ."

"So how can I grow *now*, father –" he suddenly said aloud, "– when there is no one who loves me and, worse still, no one for *me* to love?"

His throat ached with suppressed tears. Silently he begged his father to give him the courage and determination he would need to make a new and meaningful life for himself in this country Izak had so admired.

Above him the cries of the wheeling gulls sounded to Ishmael like mocking laughter, but he shook his fist at them and shouted, "Go away! I will do it. I will!"

His own words galvanised him into action and, scrambling down to the lower deck again, he wriggled out of his exit hole.

"I'm going back to World's End," he told his father. He was aware of the irony of the inn's name, but it was the only place within reach where he knew there was food. "Also, there *must* be a proper road that goes there," he went on, "a road I can take to escape from this *dead* end. And the boy might be there again. The boy with kindness in his eyes . . ."

At this thought his heart lightened a little. He decided to continue speaking aloud and at the same time to practise his English. This, he knew, was what Izak would want.

"Practice is the only way, Ishmael," he had always said. "Practise till your *thoughts* come to you in English, till you can speak it like a native."

As he crossed the bridge to the towpath he paused for a moment to watch two black swans approaching on the canal. Their heads gracefully, regally raised, they sailed beneath him, their paddling feet hardly disturbing the surface of the water. Ishmael had never before seen black swans and with a flicker of the amusement, habitual to him in happier times, he hoped they were not omens of bad luck. But dismissing such superstitious nonsense with a shrug, he set off along the path.

He imagined a conversation with the boy at the inn, conjuring up the English words he needed, making them give shape to his thoughts, backtracking when he felt he had made a mistake and stopping now and then to search for a better word.

* * * * *

Perhaps, after all, the black swans *had* been ill-omens, for his return to the World's End yielded only scanty gleanings from the bins. In desperation, he had taken the abandoned remains of someone's meal from a table and as he stuffed them into his rucksack had been spotted by a man who drove him away with curses. He had seen no sign of the boy. Since returning to his refuge in the hulk he had rationed the food he'd brought back, nibbling small amounts as it became more and more mouldy and unpalatable.

During the daylight hours there seemed to be many more people about: there were walkers and cyclists on the canal path and across the river he could see families strolling on the quayside beneath the high church wall. One day when the tide was full a motor launch steamed up the river; its deck was crowded with people and its wake, striking the wreck, shivered its ancient timbers. He wondered if all this activity signified some kind of English holiday, but that seemed odd in early winter. Afraid of encountering other people he spent the days observing them from his hiding place, dozing and dreaming until, driven by boredom and the need for food, he left it at dusk to scavenge for anything dropped by the visitors.

On the third night, exhausted by hunger, he fell into a rare deep sleep and was woken by a series of explosions in the town. In sudden terror he jolted upright as memories flooded in: memories of gunfire, of shells spinning out of the night sky and of fire and fury all around them as he and Izak fled from yet another attack. He clutched his head in his arms, rocking on his rushy bed, his heart thudding in his ears, until the warlike noises miraculously stopped and the sudden silence was broken by the sound of clapping and people singing.

Cautiously, he climbed to the upper deck, from where he could see people milling about on the waterside, cheering as fireworks bloomed like flowers in the night sky. Farther upriver, where the fields began, flames were leaping high in the air and Ishmael could hear the sort of murmur made by a large, peaceful crowd gathered together in one place. The smell of barbecuing food sneaked towards him across the water and he understood that whatever was happening in the town, it was not to do with lamentation but with celebration.

Unable to stand the tormenting smell of food, Ishmael returned to his bed. He was racked by the need for both food and fire. The nights were cruelly cold and he had no covering other than the clothes he wore and the pile of rushes into which he burrowed but which gave no comfort.

The noise from the town went on. He could hear music, a band playing and then the sound of a single guitar accompanied again by singing. He was reminded of the campfires where he and his father had sometimes met with other wayfarers: the shared food, the laughter, the twanging of stringed instruments, the throb of drums, the bursts of song – and better than all of that, the warmth of Izak's body pressed against his own.

The yearning for his father triggered by this memory plunged him into other darker recollections and throughout the fourth day, while the town returned to quietness and the November wind moaned through the cracks and muttered in the crannies of his shelter, Ishmael relived his childhood.

Pictures reeled unstoppably through his head: the repeated flights from local wars and skirmishes; the border barriers constantly raised against them; the threats and thievery by hooded men with guns; the seizures and imprisonments by uniformed men with guns; the taunts of children armed with stones; the feral dogs that menaced them; the town dogs that were set upon them; the burning days in the deserts; the icy nights in the mountains; the attacks by bandits in the wilderness, and in the cities the trickeries of wily 'entrepreneurs' who, under the guise of trying to help, exploited them for their own profit. He also remembered – worse than all these, perhaps – the squalid over-crowded camps from which escape was almost impossible and where only despair and diseases thrived.

Eventually, as the day waned, he was recalled to the present only by the imagined reproving words of his father, whose optimism rarely failed him and whose faith in the ultimate goodness of humanity had always somehow survived.

"Go back to your happier memories, my son," Izak would have said. "They are just as valid and will give you both comfort and courage. Concentrate, not on the cruelties we have suffered, but on the kindnesses – the frequent kindnesses – shown to us by many of those we have encountered on this journey. Remember how people, often themselves amongst the poorest and most powerless, have shared with us their food, their songs, their stories and their laughter."

Ishmael *did* remember, and in doing so he resolved to feel (as he knew his father had felt) that although the scales of good and evil are not evenly balanced in this world, as long as one good man remains, evil will not gain the final victory.

Long before the end of this fourth day his scraps of food had completely run out. For twenty-four hours he had eaten nothing and had drunk dry the dregs of the puddle that had so far sustained him. He realised that if he stayed in the hulk any longer he would lose the last little strength he had. For the sake of his father's dreams and for the sake of his own life, the life his father had treasured, he had to move on.

Early the next morning, while the town was still asleep, Ishmael shrugged his bag on to his shoulders and left the hulk. This time, when he reached the towpath, instead of turning left towards World's End, he turned right and began to walk wearily but steadily in the opposite direction.

III   THE COTTAGE

It was with a shock of surprise that Ishmael came upon the cottage. It stood midway between the canal and the river and although it was less than a kilometre from the Old Hulk, the lie of the land had made it invisible from the wreck. Part of the canal here was enclosed by lock gates, but unlike those at World's End these were rusting and seemed long out of use. Desperate with hunger, Ishmael wondered if he could beg a crust of bread from whoever lived in the house. Warily he crossed the small footbridge over the canal and made his way down a narrow track that led him past the cottage and on down to the riverside.

Here a rickety wooden structure jutted out across the mud and facing it on the far side he could see a much sturdier stone jetty. A sheet of paper pinned to a rotting post drew his attention and he stepped onto planks slimed with green weed to look at it. His reading of English was slow, his work with Izak having been mainly oral, and much of the lettering on the notice had been worn away by the weather. It took him some time to decipher that this was a landing place for a boat that regularly plied to and from the town and that it cost one English pound to be ferried across the river.

This morning the tide was far out, the river hardly more than a stream winding through the mud and clearly no boat could come over until the water returned. With a sigh Ishmael turned away and went back to look at the cottage.

As he wandered round it, he decided it was so small and quaint it was more like a child's play-house than a proper dwelling. The cottage was built mostly of stone but on the side overlooking the river there was a huge brick chimney which seemed designed to support the whole of its northern wall before it reached the roof and dwindled to a short chimney stack. Squinting in the strong light from the brightening sky, he peered up at this but could detect no smoke. Indeed, the whole place had an utterly deserted air. Overgrown shrubs crowded against its walls and between it and the river there was a square of lawn that looked as if it had not been cut for years. Beyond this the boundary wall dropped many metres straight into the riverbed.

When he reached the side of the building facing the canal he found the only door to the house. Its paint had faded and flaked away leaving the wood almost bare, and to the right of it a tiny window was so fogged with grime he could see nothing through it. Other windows, no two the same, were set higgledy-piggledy in the walls and above them the disproportionately high roof sloped steeply to the eaves.

For a few moments he lingered in the cobbled yard, looking at the tatty remains of birds' nests still clinging under the eaves, at the scatter of twigs and splatter of bird droppings on the stones below and finally, convinced that such a derelict place could not be inhabited, he tried the door. It was locked.

Disappointed, and with his stomach cramping painfully again, he retreated to the garden and sat on the wall. It was very quiet, very still. Even the sounds from the town across the water seemed muted and all he could hear was the thrum of motor traffic on the great bridge farther upstream. Among the buildings opposite him was a handsome gabled house with words painted in black letters on its pale grey walls. The letters were too far away for him to read, but he wondered if they spelled the name of another inn.

If only he could get across the river! Thinking about this (and the problem of paying for his passage when a boat arrived) he took off his backpack. Years ago his father had sewn a patch of matching fabric into its base and within it had secreted a slim pouch containing his own and his wife's wedding rings.

"Insurance," Izak had said, as his deft fingers secured the material neatly, invisibly in place. "A last resort should we ever become *that* desperate."

"I think I *am* that desperate, father," Ishmael murmured, as his own fingers searched for the hidden treasure. He had a brief vision of his father's face, his thick eyebrows arched in horror as he worked out the difference between the value of a heavy gold ring and the cost of merely crossing a river in England.

* * * * *

"Hey! Boy! What are you doing there? Trespassing in my garden!"

Ishmael had just located the rings when the voice, coming apparently from the air above him, made him leap from the wall.

"I not . . ." he stammered, twisting round to find the source of the voice. "I just . . . I do nothing . . ."

He heard the slam of the only window on this side of the house and, looking up, saw a figure disappearing from behind it. Minutes later, a man came striding across the grass. With the exception that his unkempt hair and beard were white and his figure rather short and stocky, the man bore a slight but uncanny resemblance to his father. Like Izak he had a crooked nose that had clearly once been broken, thick flyaway eyebrows and beneath them the same sort of intense dark eyes that seemed to see straight through Ishmael.

Perhaps because of this elusive likeness to his father or perhaps from an instinct born of experience, something made Ishmael feel that this man, in spite of his abrupt manner, would not harm him. Slowly he sat down again and waited as the man drew closer.

"Bless us!" said the man. "If the lad hasn't gone as white as paper. And he naturally as brown as the peat in this pot!"

He kicked at a cracked earthenware trough leaning against the wall and it at once fell apart, spilling compost.

"Where in God's name d'you hail from, boy?" he said. "You stink like a midden. And you look a wreck!"

His brusque tone was belied by the softness of his voice, but his rapid speech baffled Ishmael, who was used to Izak's measured and careful English. He understood only the last five words and with a flicker of nervous humour thought of saying he had *come* from a wreck, before the caution drummed into him by his father stopped him. Shame at the way he must appear brought a faint flush to his cheeks as the man, humming under his breath, turned on his heel.

"Come!" he said.

Without another word he began to walk back towards the cottage, beckoning Ishmael to follow him.

* * * * *

Hours later, hours marked by the steady ticking of a big white-faced clock on the wall of the room where he sat, Ishmael reflected on the extraordinary events of those hours. On the clock face were bold letters advertising the name of a train station somewhere in England and the

261

Roman numerals told him that the time was now twelve o'clock.

He was sitting on a lumpy sofa whose upholstery had lost all colour and texture. Apart from that there was only a table and one upright wooden chair in the room. An old-fashioned typewriter surrounded by tottering piles of paper took up most of the space on the table. The walls were lined with books stacked on roughly-made shelves and yet more books cluttered those parts of the stone floor that were not covered by a wrinkled, threadbare rug.

The room was dim, lit only by the small window beside the door and another, equally small, set above a bare wooden staircase. The first thing the man had done after ushering Ishmael into the house, was to thrust a garish blue and orange towel into his hands and send him up those stairs to the tiny bathroom with instructions to have a shower. While Ishmael, weeping from the joy of it, lathered himself with soap and sluiced himself with hot water, a fire had been lit in the living room and by the time he came down, dressed in a baggy crimson sweater and grey jogging pants belonging to the man, the flames were casting jittery shadows across the smoke-stained walls.

"I've put your disgusting togs to soak in a bucket," said the man. "And I've some soup heating on the stove for you. From the look of you I suspect you could devour a horse. But you'd better take it easy, or you're likely to throw up, so you are!"

Ishmael strained to understand. Surely in England nobody devoured horses? As well as being fast the man's
speech was strangely accented and he used words in ways
unfamiliar to the boy. He disappeared into the kitchen
adjacent to the living room and went on talking but,
uncertain of how much he was grasping, Ishmael said
nothing.

"Until your clothes have dried, lad," said the man,
coming back and handing him a bowl of soup in which
floated hefty chunks of carrot and other root vegetables,
"you're stuck here with me, so you are. Can you give me
a name for yourself?"

Slowly Ishmael swallowed a mouthful of the hot, tasty
soup. He thought of the common English names his father
had suggested they use when they arrived in England, and
without looking at the man he said, "Is Smith . . . my name
is John Smith."

The man laughed. "Sure it is!" he said. "And mine's
Luke Skywalker!"

Ishmael knew he was not believed but to his surprise
the man did not press him. Instead he said quietly, "Right.
So. John it is. But you'd better be calling me Donal . . ."

In the following hour while Ishmael finished a second
bowl of soup and fretted about the false name he had
given, Donal sat on the wooden chair beside the table and
talked. At some point he left his chair and lowered him-

self on to the rug beside the sofa where Ishmael sat silently staring into the fire.

"Sure, you're about as communicative as yon lads," said Donal. He pointed to a picture where two boys in long-ago clothes sat entranced as they listened to a grizzled seafaring man, who seemed to be telling them a story. "Are you understanding me at all, John?"

Ishmael nodded, though in truth Donal's voice, low and dreamy (almost as if he were talking to himself) was lulling him to sleep. Between moments of absence he picked up that Donal had: 'escaped from trouble' in Ireland when very young; studied at an English university; married a girl he met there; taught in both schools and colleges, and lived in a large number of places. He had never had children of his own and it was only when his wife had died five years ago that he had come to live in the lock-keeper's cottage.

"There you have it then, John," he was saying as Ishmael surfaced again. "My life in the proverbial nutshell. I have to tell you the folk just across the river there think I'm a mad kind of a fellow! They say I live alone in this godforsaken place because I have some dark, disgraceful secret to hide. Sure, that's not it. Not it at all! Isn't the reason I'm here as innocent as your own?"

He hesitated on a laugh and then went on.

"The fact is, for the better part of my life I've had to be earning my living by teaching young scamps like you to love books. But my dream has always been to write a book myself, so it has! And it's the pension for all those years of service that's let me take refuge at last in this peaceful place between the waters. Here I can read and think and write without interruption and no-one – except maybe a rare wandering boy like yourself – can just drop in on me!"

The clock on the wall was saying five by the time Donal stood up, stretched with a groan and returned to his kitchen. Ten minutes later he came back with two thick slices of bread and a long-handled fork. He stirred the fire with a poker until the flames died down, and then squatting before it he fixed each slice in turn on the fork and held it close to the glowing embers. As the enticing smell of toasting bread filled the room he glanced over his shoulder at Ishmael.

"Sure, and haven't I rattled on long enough," he said, "to put any lad into a stupor – especially one I'd say has not slept properly for many a night?"

They ate the toast with poached eggs followed by a slice of fruit cake and a large mug of tea. Ishmael tried to apologize for his sleepiness and silence.

"Sorry I not talk," he said. "My father teach me English very good but . . ."

"But your brain's banjaxed by exhaustion," said Donal. "Not to worry. Tomorrow, maybe it's yourself can do the talking."

It was half-statement, half-question and without waiting for a response, he started to clear away their plates.

He disappeared again into his kitchen where Ishmael could hear him filling a kettle and a few minutes later he returned and, raising Ishmael's legs so that he was lying full length among the cushions on the sofa, he covered him with a blanket.

"Sleep," he said.

Then, carrying another, even larger mug of tea, he hummed his way up the stairs.

Silence fell on the house. Beyond the soothing tick of the clock Ishmael could hear the swish and patter of rain on the windows, the sigh of wind through the nearby trees and farther off, the bleating of sheep on the marshland. Warmth enveloped him and sleep, at last, swept him away.

* * * * *

Some hours passed swiftly, some dragged, as over the next three days Ishmael slept less and ate more. The food Donal cooked was good but strange to him; omelettes, potatoes baked in their skins, pastas with tomato and onion or creamy mushroom sauces, vegetables steamed and then grilled under a layer of cheese.

"No flesh of any kind," said Donal, "has passed these lips for many years."

"Where . . . how . . . you get this food?" Ishmael asked him.

"Don't I fetch it my own self?" said Donal. "From the town over yonder."

"On the ferry boat?"

"Bless you, no. Nowadays those fellows only operate when the holidaymakers are here. But I have my own little cockleshell down below there."

He nodded in the direction of the river.

Ishmael puzzled over 'cockleshell' and decided it must be some sort of boat. He wondered if, with two instead of one to feed, Donal's stocks were running low, but he seemed in no hurry to fetch more – or for Ishmael to leave. The rain that had begun the night of his arrival at the cottage continued to fall and Donal claimed he could not get Ishmael's clothes dried.

"Sure, haven't they hung on my line for days and aren't they just as sodden as when I pulled them from the bucket?"

Meanwhile, he lent Ishmael another sweater and sometimes tried to coax him to talk about his own past.

Well-trained by Izak to be careful of what he said about himself, Ishmael told him as little as possible. He never told Donal where he had come from nor where he had actually travelled. He said nothing at all about the accident that had brought him to the lock-keeper's cottage and did not mention his time in the Old Hulk. He said only that his mother had died when he was very young and that he and his father had lived in many places until his father too had died while on his way to England.

"Was it your Da's profession that sent you on your travels?" said Donal.

"My father was teacher," said Ishmael, avoiding a direct answer. "Like you."

"You mean your Da taught English?"

"No. He study English for long time, but he teach science in university. He teach about the weather . . ."

"He'd be just the man for this country then," said Donal, "for don't we have an excess of *that* here?"

This talk of his father had brought a rush of pain to Ishmael and his eyes stung with tears.

"I think," said Donal gently, for Ishmael was rocking to and fro in a childlike motion of distress, "it might be 'climatology' you mean, John. The study of worldwide weather systems. Would it be the business of our rapidly changing climate your Da was concerned with?"

Ishmael gave him a wan smile and said, yes, it was.

Donal had not seen a newspaper in years, had no television in the cottage and used his radio mostly for listening to music. From other sources he was nevertheless well informed about the threat posed by climate change. He knew nothing of the tragic event responsible for Ishmael's arrival at his door but, from occasional news bulletins he *had* heard, he knew that refugees, mainly from Africa and Asia, were trickling into the country. Privately, he suspected that changes were taking place in the world's moral climate too; that the increase everywhere in dishonesty, corruption, fanaticism, brutality and barbarity were threatening the moral consensus by which civilised societies attempted to live; and that these geophysical and moral changes were somehow interconnected and would eventually turn this trickle into an unstoppable flood.

"Sure, and isn't climate change the very thing we should all – every man, woman and child of us – be studying now?" he said. "Yet the whole world shies away from it, pays it lip service and little else while we charge like suicidal lemmings towards a cliff edge . . ."

Donal's voice had become passionate, and Ishmael stopped rocking.

"My father think that too," he said. "He think it mightily!"

Donal laughed.

"What I say – it not right?" asked Ishmael.

"Sure," said Donal. "It was better than right."

Ishmael studied his face, trying to work out what he meant.

At times Donal still reminded him of his father: the way he fell quickly and naturally into teaching mode and his troubled concern over serious matters (including this particular one which he shared with Izak). Donal was less stern than his father, his manner of speaking was less didactic and he slid more easily into laughter. But then, Ishmael reflected, Donal had probably suffered less . . .

* * * * *

Overnight a gale blew in from the sea. It tossed the mewling gulls about the sky, clattered the loose tiles on the roof and shrieked down the chimney. Out in the yard Ishmael's clothes were blowing on the line, the legs of his jeans like those of a boneless ghost, folding and unfolding in a crazy dance.

He felt restless. The warmth of the cottage, the comfort of the couch where he slept, the pleasure of the food and above all, Donal's company and kindness, were restoring his energy but robbing him of purpose. He knew he could not stay and yet had no plan for escape until this morning an idea suddenly surfaced – an idea that had been lurking in his subconscious since his discovery that Donal had a boat. What if he were to 'borrow' that boat and cross on his own to the town?

Donal was upstairs writing. He insisted on keeping to his routine of writing for three hours every morning, taking notepads, pens, pencils and a flask of coffee up to his bedroom.

"I need to be on my own, lad," he said apologetically. "I always do the first draft the old-fashioned way – by hand – and even your quiet company would be a distraction."

By this time he was probably lost in a world of his own making, humming as his pen stuttered across the page. On impulse, Ishmael slipped out of the door. The gale snatched it and banged it shut. He held his breath but there was no response from inside the house. Instead of crossing the garden where he knew the drop from the boundary wall was too far for him to jump, he made his way to the path that went down to the ferry's landing place.

From there he could hear the eerie whistling of the wind in the rigging of the boats in the boatyard and the metallic chorus of halyards striking the masts. The tide was receding and between where he stood and the water's edge the ridges of exposed mud had been sculpted into wave-like patterns. He could see Donal's boat lying in its small inlet among the reeds but realised at once that it would be too heavy for him to drag as far as the water. Moreover, as he watched the turbulent flow of the outgoing tide, he was struck by a surge of terror at the thought of setting foot in a boat. The night when the sea had flung him on to the shores of this alien land, the night it had stolen his father, recurred over and over again in his dreams, constantly disturbing his sleep even in this safe haven.

"Hey, Johnnie!"

Johnnie was the name Donal had taken to calling him by, and Ishmael no longer hesitated at its unfamiliarity. He swung round and saw the man approaching him along the path. He looked like a great black bird as the waterproof cloak he was wearing billowed and flapped in the gale.

"You weren't thinking of going for a swim, I hope!" he shouted.

Ishmael shook his head and began to climb back towards him.

"No," he said. "I just look at the town."

"Hard to believe it was once an important port, isn't it?" said Donal, shading his eyes from a sudden flare of sunlight. "Sure, I should be working but I couldn't resist coming out to see the world being turned topsy-turvy by the weather!"

He led the way back, but instead of turning for the cottage continued as far as the canal where he crossed the bridge on to the towpath. The sun disappeared again behind scudding clouds and the wind hissed over the reeds, shaking their pale feathery heads and then flattening their stalks so that it seemed as if a tidal wave had swept over them. In the marshes beyond them cattle were grazing, and Ishmael could see a network of trails that meandered everywhere but seemed to lead nowhere. From the trees on the knoll to his left a battalion of rooks rose, cawing in protest as the branches where they roosted were shaken by a savage gust.

Donal began to stroll in the direction of the hulk. Long before they reached it, he halted and pointed towards the hills.

"Once upon a time," he said, "when the city upstream was still the thriving port for this region, a rich and powerful woman lived over yonder. She owned all the land hereabouts as well as the harbour rights for this town, which meant the taxes and tallies on any goods unloaded here went into *her* capacious pockets!"

"So," said Ishmael, who sensed a good story coming. "What happen?"

"Well, didn't the owld witch have great stone weirs built just a few miles upriver from here?" said Donal. "And didn't they block entirely the passage of ships to the city's own port?"

"And that mean ships have to . . . have to . . ." Ishmael stopped. He had grasped the situation but could not find the word he needed next.

"Aye, right enough," said Donal. "They had to dock *here* instead. Making this place the major port. And herself wealthier than ever."

They were both silent for a moment, contemplating the craftiness of such an act, the wickedness of the rich and powerful.

"Hey, ho!" said Donal at last. "That's the way of the world, Johnnie. But the city fathers didn't accept defeat. They brought in engineers from Wales – and from wherever they could find experts on waterway construction – to build this canal and bypass her pesky weirs." He stood

273

humming a tuneless little sequence of notes and then laughed. "Or that was the idea," he said.

"But it not work?" said Ishmael.

As Donal began explaining to him in some detail why the plan had not really succeeded, Ishmael's attention drifted, caught by the sight of a bird standing at the water's edge only a few metres away. It was so still that its long spindly legs seemed rooted to the spot, its curved neck and pale grey body giving its silhouette an 'S' shape that, but for the ruffling of its plumage by the wind, might have been carved out of stone. He was about to draw Donal's attention to it when he heard him say something about the canal locks being the first ever used in Britain.

"There are four altogether," he was saying. "And four lock-keeper's houses – including my own darlin' little place and the much grander one that's turned itself into a pub at World's End."

Ishmael still did not want to admit he had been to World's End but, puzzled by the name, he asked why it was called that.

"Sure, doesn't it stand where both river and canal disappear into the sea," said Donal, "with nothing beyond it but wind and water?"

"Lot of wind and water here, too," observed Ishmael, turning in a circle as the breeze snatched his long hair and blew it across his face. His movement disturbed the bird which rose on wide wings and with trailing legs just skimming the trees, vanished into the grey light.

"Hah!" exclaimed Donal. "I hadn't noticed that old heron was here with us."

The cold was biting through yet another sweater of Donal's that Ishmael was wearing, and he shivered. Donal noticed and suggested they should not go any farther.

"This path go all way from World's End to city?" said Ishmael as they turned.

"Right," said Donal.

"You can walk there? To city?"

"You can," said Donal. "But it's a fearsome long trek, so it is. Much easier to cross the river and catch a bus!"

"It very lonely here," said Ishmael, as they crossed the bridge.

"Haven't I been telling you, Johnnie? I *like* lonely. And I like simple too. I try to live like the old keepers of this place did – without any modern contraptions. Sure, where in my hobbit-hole would I put such things anyway?"

Ishmael, regretting the loss of the cell-phone that Izak had carried, pointed out that a telephone did not need space.

Donal snorted and dismissed telephones as intrusive and – by all accounts nowadays – frequently *abusive* too.

"The fact is, Johnnie," he said, "if we're going to avoid that rush to the *real* end of the world, we're all going to have to get used to 'simple' again, so we are!"

* * * * *

November was drawing to a close. The wind abated and the weather turned calm, cold and still. The skies cleared and at night under the winking stars the cries of owls echoed across the wilderness. By morning there were slivers of ice at the river's edge and the grass was weighted with frost. Sometimes they heard the long, warbling call of a curlew or the honking of geese flying over to their feeding grounds.

Donal's store of logs in the lean-to outhouse had dwindled to half its size and instead of retreating to his bedroom to work he stayed in the warm living room, typing up his manuscript, the clickety-clack of the typewriter keys masking the quiet tick of the clock.

Whenever he stopped working he encouraged Ishmael to talk, and the boy could feel the improvement in his command of English. He was becoming easy with the language, even at times, fluent. Donal was patient, made him do exercises in pronunciation and occasionally, but firmly, corrected the mistakes in his grammar.

When alone, Ishmael began to amuse himself by mimicking Donal's own speech. He had picked up on the tags with which Donal often began or ended a sentence. "You're a grand boy, Johnnie, so you are," he murmured to himself, or "Sure, and aren't you the idiot making such an error?" In his own voice the phrases made him giggle but they were without mockery. Each day his respect and affection for the man deepened.

He knew Donal was troubled, uncertain what to do about him; that he did not want to send Ishmael out alone into a harsh and often dangerous world but neither did he want to hand him over to the 'proper authorities' without Ishmael's consent. The boy decided that, although both fuel and food were running low, Donal was delaying the necessary trip across to the town because when he went he would have to take Ishmael with him.

About all this Ishmael had guessed correctly but another factor, unknown to him, lay at the heart of Donal's inaction. Deeply buried but powerful, it arose from Donal's own history. He had been much the same age as Ishmael when his mother died and when his father, unable to cope, had first neglected him and then, increasingly under the influence of drink, had become brutally cruel.

Donal had fled and for months had wandered the streets, living by whatever means he could until he was 'adopted' by a street gang of older boys. Ruthless and lawless they had used and abused him. On the anniversary of his mother's death he had been attempting, on their behalf, to burgle the house of an elderly man who caught him in the act. But instead of handing him over to the police, the man had kept him, fed him and eventually had sent him to England to be cared for and educated by his niece and her family. It was Donal's lifelong gratitude to them that now dictated his treatment of Ishmael.

As the days went by he dithered, unsure how or where to begin with a rescue plan for the boy. In the long, quiet hours of the night, when hard frosts made the house tick and creak and laid a thickening layer of ice on the canal, he thought about it. Meanwhile, hoping to build up Ishmael's physical strength as well as to improve his language skills, he insisted on them taking 'walks with talks'. In the dramatic sunsets and smoky twilights of the late afternoons, when other people had retired to the light and warmth of an evening at home, they walked as far as the hulk; watched, laughing, as surprised ducks slid and skidded on the icy surface of the canal; crunched across the frozen grass of a circular track through the marshes; marvelled over the aerial dance of the starlings returning to roost there.

Frustrated by Ishmael's continued failure to reveal anything significant about his past or ever to explain how he came to arrive at the lock-keeper's cottage, Donal nevertheless learnt a number of things about him from these conversations. Among them was the overwhelming reverence he had for England; a reverence clearly inspired by his father.

"Be careful, Johnnie," he warned. "England is not paradise! And the big cities are especially dangerous to a boy like yourself, so they are! If you take the wrong path, or get involved with the wrong people, you could fall prey to rogues as villainous as any you've encountered anywhere else in the world . . ."

Ishmael looked grave and then grinned. His face, lit by the last golden gleams of the setting sun, looked for the first time boyishly free of care.

"Mr. Donal," he said, "you sound just like my father. *He* say those things too."

* * * * *

During the long dark evenings, with the fire rekindled and supper over, Ishmael and Donal listened to music on the radio or played chess (though Donal had not played for years and Ishmael – taught long ago by Izak – was also rusty). Sometimes they looked together at the few simple books Donal had sorted out to help Ishmael improve his reading of English, but Ishmael soon tired of these as he thought them childish. The book he preferred was an illustrated one of European birds. He had begun to take an interest in the birds he saw on the walks with Donal, and now he studied the pictures of those he recognised, trying to memorize their individual features and to learn their names.

At the very end of the day, as they sat drinking their last cup of tea, Donal had started to read aloud to him from a book he said *he* had loved when he was Ishmael's age.

"Sure," he said, "isn't *Kidnapped* a grand story? And it's a story similar to your own Johnnie – being that of a runaway, orphaned boy."

When, at the beginning, Ishmael complained about the difficult, old-fashioned English, Donal did not set the book aside but slowed his reading down, pausing it now and then to explain and interpret. Fidgety and impatient at first, Ishmael gradually found himself being drawn into the adventures of David Balfour and looking forward to the next instalment.

* * * * *

In the end it was the problem of supplies that forced the issue of what was to happen next. On the day Donal decided that if they were not to starve he could leave it no longer before making a trip into the town, the tide would be at the full by late afternoon. Even then he left it until midday before he sat Ishmael down to tell him what he planned.

Quickly realising from his unease what Donal was about to say, Ishmael felt his heart sink. He had known this day would come, must come, but increasingly unable to face the thought of it he had constantly pushed it to the back of his mind.

"You take me . . ?" he asked.

"Of course," said Donal.

"No, I mean to say . . . you take me to *police*?"

"Of course *not*!" said Donal. "You should know me better than that by now, Johnnie! But you and I, we *both* need help and advice . . . so after doing the messages today, we're going to see a friend of mine. The poor fellow's disabled and stuck at home now, but he *was* a lawyer. He's a humane and generous fellow, and you needn't be fearing he'll just hand you over . . ."

Ishmael, troubled, shook his head but said nothing.

"We'll go mid-afternoon on the incoming tide," said Donal. "The rowing's easier when the tide's just right. If you gather up your togs and pack your bag, we'll try to finish that game of chess we started last night, have a slap-up lunch to finish the rations, and go!"

By now Ishmael was back in his own clothes. Everything had been washed, and even his rags of underwear had been hung out in the yard to dry. The frost had made them as stiff as cardboard cut-outs before Donal brought them in and arranged them on a folding rack (which for some mysterious reason he called a 'clothes horse') and set them around the fire. Ishmael gathered them up and stuffed them into his backpack to join the two books Donal had given him. One was the bird book he loved, the other was *Kidnapped*. He knew that on his own, he would struggle to read this (his reading still lagged far behind his speaking) but he was touched by the gift and determined to finish it.

Outside, the frost had thawed but a sharp cold wind was blowing up from the north and the overcast sky was an oppressive yellowish grey, the colour of an old bruise. When they sat down at the chessboard, Ishmael's mind was not on the game but on the urgent questions that gnawed at him. Should he leave one of his gold rings in payment to Donal for his hospitality? And should he take this last chance to escape and sneak out while Donal was preparing the meal? He was much stronger now and was sure he could reach the city by the towpath walk.

The answer to each question came up as 'no'. In the days spent at the cottage he had come to regard Donal as a sort of shadow father. He could not insult him with an offer of payment, much less worry him by running away – and without proper thanks too! It would be a betrayal of the man's generosity, his care and concern for Ishmael. Moreover, his real father would have been grieved at such ungrateful behaviour from his son.

His lack of concentration meant the game ended quickly when Donal, with a shout of triumph, trapped his king. They lingered over their lunch of lentil soup followed by beans on toasted stale bread, and when Donal disappeared upstairs Ishmael checked that his precious rings were still securely stowed in their secret hiding place. Then, tucking his bag among the cushions on the sofa, he went out into the yard.

For one bewildered moment he thought Donal must he shaking a pillow out of the upper window, releasing thousands of feathers that were falling all around the house.

In the long years of their wandering he and Izak had never encountered snow except in distant visions of white-capped mountains, and it took him a second to realise that *this* was snow. Intrigued and excited, he returned to the house and took his anorak from the hook beside the door. The flakes were thickening, filling the air, deceiving his eyes by seeming simultaneously to spiral upwards and float down before they touched the ground and vanished. He stuck out his tongue to catch their delicate, icy prickle and ran up the bank to stand on the bridge over the canal. Here the air scoured his face, making it ache with cold. The marshes were invisible, blotted out by the blizzard, and turning from the thrust of the wind he set off along the towpath, skipping like a child for the sheer novelty of it.

Later he could not remember how far he went or for how long he stayed out there – only that when he grew tired, slowed down and turned round, he could not see the cottage at all. The snow was starting to settle, whitening the grass on the canal banks and wiping out his footsteps behind him. In sudden alarm he realised he had been away some time. Donal would be wondering where he was and fretting because they needed to set off before the power of the inrushing tide grew too strong and made the crossing difficult.

* * * * *

The door of the cottage was ajar, wind-driven snow piling up in a wedge on the flagstones inside. The house felt cold and empty and Ishmael could hear no sound of Donal upstairs. He wondered if his friend had gone out to look for him, but his duffle coat was still on its hook. As he went farther into the room, he shouted Donal's name. There was no answer. With no firelight and with the snow masking the small windows, the room was dark. As Ishmael felt his way round the end of the sofa he saw what he thought was a bundle of clothes heaped at the foot of the staircase. He moved closer and realised with shock that it was Donal himself lying there. Crumpled and inert, he lay with his feet halfway up the stairs and his head resting on the cold stones of the floor.

With a cry, Ishmael sprang towards him and crouched down, saying his name over and over as he raised his head and cradled it on his lap. There was still no movement from Donal and Ishmael's first thought (quickly dismissed, for was this not England?) was that someone had entered the house and murdered him.

In his short life he had seen many dead bodies, victims of terrorism, of war, of famine and of pestilence, and so the idea of a lifeless body did not frighten him. What *did* scare him, was that he did not know what to do, and what upset him was the thought that this was a man he had come to love; a man who had been unstintingly kind to him and who might still be alive if only Ishmael had not gone out when he did . . .

Amid the havoc of these emotions he tried to picture what Izak would have done, and the thought of his father seemed to steady his heart rate. He slid his fingers down to Donal's wrist and felt for his pulse, weeping with relief when he found one. Donal, however, still could not be roused and Ishmael saw now that he had a great swelling just beneath his hairline, a blackening bruise where his head must have struck the floor when he tumbled down the stairs.

* * * * *

Sobbing for breath, slithering on the snow-slippery path, Ishmael staggered down to the river. He had been afraid of trying to move Donal in case he did him more harm, and so had placed a cushion under his head and covered him with blankets before leaving him. When he reached the water's edge he waded through the reeds to the inlet where Donal's boat was securely moored to an iron ring in the enclosing wall. He slung his backpack into it and with freezing fingers struggled to untie the rope. He heard himself praying aloud to God for strength, to Izak for courage and to Donal that he should stay alive.

The tide was not yet quite full but flowing strongly, the water already swishing round his feet. At last he released the knot and dragging at the bows of the boat felt it lift as the waves seized it, threatening to tug it out of his grasp. Clumsy with fear, he pitched himself over the side and clambered on to the seat as the dinghy rocked and veered and the oars in the bottom clattered from side to side. Somehow he managed to pick them up and fumble them into the rowlocks, terrified of dropping and losing one.

"Help me, help me," he sobbed, as the boat spun without control, water leaping around it, slapping against the hull and slopping over the gunwales. But there was no-one to hear, let alone help. Across the water, through the drifting snow, he could just discern the pale walls of the inn Donal called 'the owld Ferryman' and downriver he could see the lights of other dwellings, blurrily reflected in the rapidly-moving water.

As the boat bobbed aimlessly on the waves, he at last fixed the oars in position. Ishmael had never rowed a boat and knew only the shape of the movements involved. He found the oars were heavy and awkward and when he dipped them into the water, one or both seemed momentarily to get caught in a steel trap. The river snatched at him, turning him in circles as it thrust him into the tide's onward rush, sweeping him up the river and away from where he needed to be.

He had no idea how long it took him, but after a while he found a rhythm and discovered also that by using one oar on its own he could manoeuvre the craft in the direction he wanted. Grunting with the effort, he at last succeeded in turning the boat back. Pushing against the force of the tide was hard, punishing work and his hands were growing sore from the friction. But the snow was easing and perhaps his prayers were being answered for the river seemed suddenly to hesitate and then settle beneath him. Moments later, instead of impeding him, the now receding tide was aiding him as he worked his way back to where he could again see The Ferryman Inn.

Dusk had deepened into darkness and the inn was brightly lit, the town beyond it sketched out in points of light. The relief of gaining some control made Ishmael laugh, though his blistered hands were frozen to the oars, his eyelashes crusted with snow and his face rigid with cold. Painfully he steered closer to the bank and felt another change as the dinghy freed itself from the current of the main channel. Almost as if it knew its own way it slid past the pub and glided into calm water. He rested the oars and let the river carry him round a shallow bend before it ran him aground on a widening margin of dry land. A short distance away he saw the high wall that surrounded the church and beneath it the quayside where, from his first refuge in the hulk, he had watched people strolling.

Stunned by his success in reaching the land, Ishmael sat blowing on his hands, his head bowed in thanks. Slowly, stiffly, he removed the oars from the rowlocks, laid them in the bottom of the boat and picked up his bag. Then he climbed out. His feet sank deep into thick, gloopy mud and he held on to the gunwales, fearful of sinking altogether. Across the river the old wreck was merely a patch of deeper shadow against the darkness of the bank and further upstream the lock-keeper's cottage, with no lights in its windows, was invisible.

A few flakes of snow twirled lazily down and, re-assured by now that the mud was not going to swallow him, he began, one wearisome step at a time, to make for the jetty that led up to the quayside. There was nobody about. The snow had settled in a thin mantle on roofs and walls and more thickly on the road. His feet slurred through it, his legs threatening to give way, as he stumbled along a dark alleyway between tall warehouses, his whole being focussed on the lights at the end of it.

The lights of The Ferryman Inn.

IV   THE FERRYMAN INN

Although it was still only late afternoon, the inn was busy. Sounds of talk and laughter from within reached Ishmael minutes before he collapsed against the door. There was a brief pause in the racket as he slipped down the surface of the door and crumpled on the doormat. His anorak hood had snagged on something and he could feel the round brass doorknob twist against his shoulder as someone turned it from inside. The door eased open and he went with it until he lay with his head inside the pub and his feet stretched out in the snow.

"Good God!" a man's voice exclaimed. "What have we here?"

Incapable of speech, Ishmael said nothing, staring helplessly up into a pair of bright blue eyes that, wide with astonishment, stared back into his. The eyes were deep set, fanned about with wrinkles, and as the whole face came closer, he saw that a man of about the same age as Donal was stooping over him, his eyes now full of concern.

"Help," he whispered. "Help . . . Donal . . ."

The man squatted, raised Ishmael's head and propped him against his legs.

"Say again, lad," he said.

"Donal," repeated Ishmael. "Donal . . . hurt . . ."

The man shouted something into the interior of the pub and then lifted Ishmael, carrying him into the bar where half a dozen people, drinks in hands, stood silently watching them. A hubbub broke out and several of them surged forward to help.

"He's soaking, freezing . . ."

"Must have fallen in the river . . ."

"Or the mud. Look at his legs . . ."

"Whatever! He needs to be stripped and wrapped in warm blankets or he's in danger of hypothermia. Anyone recognise him? Know who he is?"

The voices circled, clamoured. Ishmael, all his senses blunted by cold and the desire to sleep, could make no sense of any of their words. The man, still carrying him pushed his way through the others to where a fire burned in a wide hearth and laid him on a rug in front of it.

"Fetch Sally," he said to someone. "I'm not sure, but I think the boy said Donal's in trouble. Hurt. Can you find Jack and get him to go across to the cottage? And tell him to take someone with him in case he needs help."

There was more bustle and shouting and the sound of doors slamming. The blue-eyed man leaned over him and somebody else, somebody he could not see, chaffed his icy hands.

"Did you say *Donal*?" said this person. "That Donal is *hurt*?"

"Fell," said Ishmael, dazed and drifting into uncon-sciousness and unable to find the English words he needed.

"In the house or outside?"

"Inside . . . on . . . on *stairs*."

Both men groaned and the unseen one said, "Daft old bugger, living alone over there in that hovel! Without even a phone! He's been an accident waiting to happen. Could've had a stroke . . . a heart-attack . . . anything. And no-one would know. . ."

The men stood up as a woman came to their side.

"Who is he?" she asked, looking closely at Ishmael. "Is he a relative of Donal's?"

"No idea. The boy can hardly speak. But I shouldn't think so. All that can wait, though. We probably need to call an ambulance for when Jack comes back with the old man. Meanwhile the priority here must be this lad. Can we take him upstairs, Sally? Dunk him in a hot bath? We can get more information out of him later."

* * * * *

It was later – but how much later Ishmael could not tell. He had been stripped of his clothes, placed in a warm bath, left to soak and then vigorously rubbed dry with a hot towel by the woman they called Sally.

"No need to be embarrassed," she told him briskly when she noticed his discomfiture. "I'm used to boys. I've a son of about your age."

She enfolded him in a quilt and took him into a small room with crooked walls and smoke-blackened wooden beams where she sat him in a deep armchair beside the fire.

"We're in the Snug," she told him. "It's a private part of the house and you won't be bothered by anyone here."

While she busied herself adding coal to the fire and tidying mugs and papers from the table, she told Ishmael she was the wife of the innkeeper; that the two fishermen who had gone across to Donal's cottage had found him alive but still unconscious; that they had brought him back and he was on his way to the city hospital; that it was just as well that he, Ishmael, had arrived when he did because it had started to snow heavily again; and that everyone was dying to hear his story when he was ready to tell it.

Later still, as he dozed, and sensation returned to his fingers and toes and sense to his head, Ishmael worried about this. How was he going to tell his story? What should he say to explain his presence here? He wanted, above all, to fulfil his father's dream and to make a life for himself in the land Izak often referred to as '*this dear land, dear for her reputation through the world*'. But was that reputation still justified? Everyone he had encountered so far had been kind, but he knew that would not always be the case. Also, there were laws governing who might be allowed to stay in England. He had no papers, no proof of who his father had been, or from what country they had come . . .

For some time Ishmael's repressed grief and longing for his father had lain dormant but now it suddenly surfaced, racking him with a pain that seemed to twist his heart in his chest. "I am too young," he cried aloud. "I cannot! I cannot do this!"

"Cannot do what?" asked Sally coming back into the room.

Ishmael straightened and shook his head. She was carrying a tray on which stood a bowl of soup and a hunk of bread. She placed the tray on a table beside him where it steamed out a hot, savoury smell, but she noted the stress on his face and the pain in his eyes, and when he stayed silent she lifted the bowl and placed it in his hands.

"Well," she said. "I hope what you *can* do is eat this. It's spicy chicken with tomato and noodles."

"Thank you," he said, suddenly realising how hungry he was. "It smell wondrous . . ."

She smiled and watched him as he began to eat. He tried hard not to gulp the soup down too fast. From below he could hear the hum of conversation, an occasional outbreak of laughter, and from outside the crunch of footsteps on snow.

"Many people come," he said. "I am . . . I am not convenient . . ."

"On the contrary," said Sally. "You're good for business, my lover. Half the town's drinking down there." Beneath her fringe of blonde hair her grey eyes shone with laughter. "We don't often get half-drowned mud-larks coming out of the river. They all want to know who you are and where you hail from."

Ishmael was about to take the last mouthful of soup but stopped with the spoon suspended in mid-air.

"Please," he said, his breath tightening with dread. "Please, I cannot . . ."

"Ah," said Sally. "I see. *That's* what you can't do . . ."

She had misunderstood his original cry of protest but now saw straight away that it had to do with his reluctance to explain himself. Her face became serious and she patted his hand.

"Not to worry," she said. "I reckon you're still in shock. But if you don't want to talk yet – at least let us have your name!"

Ishmael set the spoon down. Heat was rising into his face. He could not bear to give her the name he had given Donal and his real name was locked inside him.

"My bag," he whispered. "Where is my bag?"

Sally left his side and crossed the room to a radiator where she had hung his rucksack to dry.

"Here," she said. "It's quite safe."

She waited, expecting him to produce from it his name – or something that would identify him – but instead Ishmael clasped it to him and sat as if in a trance. She picked up his empty bowl and set it back on the tray.

"Well," she said. "Perhaps you'd like to check through your bag, quietly, on your own. But nobody has touched it except me, and I didn't open it! Don't cuddle it too closely, it's still rather damp."

She headed for the door. "I must get on," she said. "I've asked my son to find you some dry clothes. You're much the same size, I reckon. He'll bring them for you shortly. Meanwhile, try to sleep again."

* * * * *

The boy came in without knocking, startling Ishmael awake. He tried to stand up but, tangled in the duvet, failed and sank back into the chair.

"Well, blow me down!" said the boy. "If it isn't you!"

He dropped a load of garments on the floor and came closer, peering at Ishmael, shaking his head and laughing.

Ishmael stared at him, nonplussed.

"Don't you remember?" said the boy. "We've seen each other before. Yonks ago. You were scared of Dingbat. Fact is, I had the feeling you were scared of me as well as my dog. Which is a joke 'cos both of us are wimps, plus, plus!"

Yonks and wimps, plus, plus. The words defeated Ishmael, but as his eyes and brain cleared of sleep and the other boy stood grinning above him, he recognised him. He was the boy who had been at World's End: the boy who had left his salad for Ishmael to eat.

In fact, he had reappeared in Ishmael's memory many times; the bright blue eyes; the cropped straw-coloured hair; the tuft on the crown that now reminded him of the lapwing in his bird book. And the boisterous, shaggy dog.

"Where is Ding . . . the dog . . ?" he asked, suddenly shy and lost for anything to say.

The boy giggled. "Ding the Dog," he said. "I like that. He's roasting by the fire in the kitchen."

"*Roasting?*"

The alarm in Ishmael's voice made the boy laugh again. "It's a figure of speech," he said. "Dingbat likes to get as close to the fire as he can. He's fairly stupid. Wasn't named Dingbat for nothing."

He loomed over Ishmael, who felt at a disadvantage just sitting there. It seemed extraordinary to him that the lapwing boy should be here at all. Did he belong to both World's End *and* The Ferryman? As though sensing his discomfort, the boy moved back a step or two.

"Mum says you've been staying with Donal," he said. "She says you rowed his beaten-up old dinghy across to get help. What with it being dark and snowing and all . . . I reckon that was really cool!"

"Yes," said Ishmael. "*Really* cold."

The boy blinked. "Sorry," he said. "I keep forgetting your English isn't quite . . . I remember when I met you at Uncle Joe's I thought . . . I mean . . ."

Clearly unsure how Ishmael might take this implied criticism of the way he spoke, he stopped, and with a grin held out his hand in a formal way. "I'm Thomas, by the way," he said. "What's your name?"

"Ish . . ." began Ishmael, caught unawares.

"Ish?" The boy frowned as though puzzled, and repeated it again. Then, to Ishmael's astonishment, his face lit up with a sort of excited delight. "Do you mean Ish . . . mael?" he shouted. "Are you *Ishmael*?"

Taken aback by this reaction and regretting the escape of his name, Ishmael nodded.

"Wow!" said Thomas. "Wow! Jiminy fizzing Cricket! I *know* about you."

He was jumping up and down, and in a rapid gabble that again escaped Ishmael's understanding, Thomas continued, shouting, "You came in a boat . . . I don't mean tonight . . . I meant yonks . . . that is . . . *ages* ago. You were with a load of refugees who crossed the Channel in a boat even more cronky than Donal's . . . and it was wrecked just off the coast here. It was in the news, man! *You* were in the news . . ."

He left the last word hanging and dashed across the room, where he began to root about in a box beside the hearth.

"Come on," he muttered "come on, come on! Where are you? Please be here. Please don't let Mum have lit the fire with you yet."

Totally bewildered, Ishmael watched as sheets of brown paper, used envelopes, advertising flyers and old magazines flew in all directions. At last, with a cry of triumph, Thomas brandished a torn and dirty newspaper.

"Got it!" he cried. He smoothed it out on the floor, straightening the creases, brushing off dust and bits of tinder.

"Look," he said to Ishmael, his face red from excitement and the fire's heat. "Come here and look at this."

Clutching the quilt around him, Ishmael staggered up and stooped to see where Thomas was pointing. He could not take in any of the printed text, but there, in a grainy, fuzzy black-and-white photograph, he saw clearly and without any doubt, the face of his father.

* * * * *

It was Sally who explained it all to him. An hour after Thomas had called to her for help because Ishmael had fainted, she gently and very slowly read the newspaper article that described the terrible events of nearly a month ago; the events that in the end, had brought him to her door.

While Thomas fidgeted beside him, jigging about on a stool that threatened to overturn beneath him, interrupting with cries of, "I did suspect something . . . you know I did, Mum . . . I told you about the boy I met at Uncle Joe's

... the boy who was scared of Dingbat ... I knew there was something peculiar about him," Ishmael sat dumbly, tossed on a tempestuous tide of emotion that swept him from confusion to amazement, to sorrow and finally, unbelievably, to joy.

He discovered that not everyone had been lost on that night when thirty-two people were thrown into the sea, the night when Ishmael himself was cast up on the shores of England. The crew of the local lifeboat had rescued twelve people, and among them had been Izak. Clinging to the hull of the capsized boat, he had kept afloat long enough for the men to reach him. Suffering from the cold and with a serious injury to his leg, he had been concerned only for his son who had disappeared, swallowed by the sea and carried away by the erratic and powerful currents along this part of the coast. They had searched for the boy but had failed to find him.

"'Course they failed," crowed Thomas, slapping Ishmael on the back. "He was at old Donal's, wasn't he?"

"Donal should have known," murmured his mother. "News about the search for Ishmael went on for days. I can't understand why he didn't put two and two together."

"Well, he's a fizzing hermit, isn't he?" said Thomas. "Dad says he doesn't have television or newspapers or anything. And he only listens to music on his radio."

"Yes," said Ishmael "is true. But I not with Donal at start. I am hiding for many days in boat . . . in big broken boat on river bank."

"You mean the hulk!" said Thomas. "You hid in the Old Hulk! How crazy is that?"

Both Ishmael's companions stared at him in horror.

"Also," said Ishmael, "when Donal ask, I tell to him my name is John . . ."

"He can't have believed that!" said Sally. "Donal may be eccentric, but he's not stupid."

"No," said Ishmael. "He very clever! I think he *not* believe . . ."

"Perhaps he liked your company," said Thomas. "Being on his tod over there all the time he must be lonely."

"He happy with lonely," said Ishmael, "but I think he not want to put me in trouble."

"Very likely," said Sally. "Donal's kind and he's also a rebel. He wouldn't want to give the authorities the satisfaction!"

Dread nibbled once more at Ishmael. "What happen now?" he said. "My father? Is he in prison? Will I be allow to see him?"

Sally set down the newspaper.

"I'm sure you will, my lover," she said. "As far as I know your father, like Donal, is in the city hospital. I'm going to leave you both now to keep each other company while I find out more. Your father needs to know you're alive, safe and well. Later, we'll fix for you to see him. After that . . ."

She glanced at Thomas, who said nothing.

"Well," she said, "after that I honestly don't know. We shall have to see. But one thing I am sure of. Nobody's going to prison."

* * * * *

The morning light crept in under the eaves of the attic bedroom where Ishmael lay. It had a strange, intense quality that puzzled him, until he realised it came from the sun's reflection on the snow lying on an adjacent rooftop. It seemed to him that the light that today illuminated his spirit had a similar strange intensity.

Before Sally had settled him there the previous evening, she was able to tell him that Donal was conscious but suffering from concussion and two broken ribs. She also confirmed that his father was still in the hospital. She was proposing to take Ishmael to see him later in the day. She had warned him there was a long way to go yet. Without giving him any details (for she did not want to alarm Ishmael) she said only that both Izak and Ishmael would have to 'go through Immigration' before decisions were made as to whether they could stay in England.

"I reckon the signs are good, though," she said. "Apparently the authorities have been in touch with the university, who would very much like your Dad to stay.

Something to do with his important work on climate change. Meanwhile my Thomas is very keen for *you* to stay. He's revelling in being at the centre of such a drama. He wants to show you off to his friends."

Ishmael had quailed and Sally had smiled. "Well," she said, "all that can wait. But Tom, the daft boy, maintains that the way you first met at World's End and then again here at The Ferryman, means it is written in the stars that you two should be friends . . ."

Warm now under the duvet, with the light brightening both outside and within him, Ishmael listened to the softly repeated call of a bird he could see perched on a nearby chimney pot. For the first time since he lost his father he felt safe, and in the depths of himself, he felt the first stirrings of hope. Izak was alive and expected to recover. He, Ishmael, was no longer alone in the world. Whatever was to happen in the future they would be together and they had *both* made it to the land in which his father had placed such faith.

Ishmael climbed out of bed and went to the window. He looked long and hard at the bird on the chimney. Its plumage was a soft grey like the English sky, its neck feathers touched with shimmering patches of violet and pale turquoise. He found his backpack, carefully placed where he could see it on a chest of drawers. He checked again that his parent's wedding rings were securely in their hiding place and then withdrew Donal's book on birds. It was slightly damp, the cover stained, and some of the pages were wrinkled, but the colours of the illustrations inside were still clear and sharp. Returning to bed, he began to leaf through it to find the bird he had been watching.

On the stairs there was a loud, clatter of footsteps and then Thomas's voice, shouting that he was bringing up some breakfast. A proper English breakfast.

Ishmael found the bird and carefully pronounced its name aloud.

"*Pig – eon.*"

"Who you calling a pig?" demanded Thomas, banging through the door with a laden tray.

Ishmael raised the open book and showed him the picture.

"Ah!" said Thomas. "That! That's not how you say it. It's pronounced 'pidgin'."

He set the tray down across Ishmael's knees.

"Porridge in the bowl," he said. "With brown sugar and cream. And keeping warm under this tin hat thingy there's scrambled eggs on toast . . ."

The bird outside called again and Ishmael smiled to himself. He wondered if he would ever get used to the oddities of English pronunciation or the proliferation of English metaphors.

"Mum says you must eat every last crumb," said Thomas, sinking on to the bed beside him and stealing a finger of toast.

"No problem," said Ishmael. "This morning I can eat whole *horse!*"